# POSH DOCS
## Honourable, eligible, and in demand!

Meet the Honourable Radleys:

Baron Rupert Charles
The Hon. Sebastian Henry
The Hon. Victoria

Three aristocratic doctors, the very best
in their field, who just can't avoid
the limelight!

In this exciting and emotional new
trilogy from bestselling author **Kate Hardy**
read how these eligible medics do their best
to stay single—but find love where
they least expect it…

This month in
HIS HONOURABLE SURGEON
Victoria, a hardworking and ambitious
registrar in neurology, meets her match in
new consultant Jake Lewis.

**Dear Reader**

I live in Norwich, in the east of England, with my husband, two young children, one bouncy spaniel, and too many books to count! When I'm not busy writing romance or researching local history, I help out at my children's schools; I'm a school governor and chair of the PTA. I also love cooking—see if you can spot the recipes sneaked into my books! (They're also on my website, along with extracts and stories behind the books.)

I've been writing Medical Romance™ for nearly five years now. For me, it's the best of both worlds, because I get to combine my interest in health issues with my love of good stories and romance. I really enjoy the research aspect and very emotional drama— which is why *His Honourable Surgeon* is set in the neurology department.

The Honourable Victoria Radley is far too serious to have a social life, and Jake Lewis is too busy raising money for charity in his grandmother's name to want to date. They're almost complete opposites in many ways—the posh girl and the boy next door. And they definitely don't want to fall in love. Vicky's devoted to her career, and Jake doesn't want to risk losing a family for the third time. But the attraction between them is too strong to be denied.

Then the crisis hits. Something neither of them can walk away from. When the stakes are this high, there's only one thing that will work: love. True love.

And that's exactly what Jake and Vicky find!

I'm always delighted to hear from readers, so do drop in to my website at www.katehardy.com and say hello!

*Kate*

# HIS
# HONOURABLE
# SURGEON

BY
KATE HARDY

MILLS & BOON®

For Wendy

All the characters in this book have no existence outside
the imagination of the author, and have no relation
whatsoever to anyone bearing the same name or names.
They are not even distantly inspired by any individual
known or unknown to the author, and all the incidents
are pure invention.

First published in Great Britain 2006
Large Print edition 2006
Harlequin Mills & Boon Limited,
Eton House, 18-24 Paradise Road,
Richmond, Surrey TW9 1SR

© Pamela Brooks 2006

ISBN-13: 978 0 263 18891 2
ISBN-10:      0 263 18891 4

Set in Times Roman 16 on 20 pt.
17-1106-52396

Printed and bound in Great Britain
by Antony Rowe Ltd, Chippenham, Wiltshire

DBC 21.11.06

# PROLOGUE

'ISN'T she the most gorgeous baby you've ever seen?'

Vicky cuddled her new niece and hid her grin. If anyone had told her a year ago that her middle brother would be completely besotted with a baby, she'd have laughed—Seb had been the ultimate playboy and had run a mile from children. Now he was married with a daughter. And it looked as if Chloë Victoria Radley was going to have her daddy wrapped right round her tiny little finger. 'Yes, Seb. She's lovely.'

'And Alyssa and I wondered if you'd do us a favour,' Seb continued.

Babysit? Sure—except she couldn't see him letting his daughter out of his sight for long enough! 'What?' she asked.

'Would you be her godmother?'

Godmother. It'd be the nearest Vicky would ever come to having children of her own. Her older brothers might be happily married and settled down, but it wasn't for her. She didn't have time to be a wife and mother—not if she wanted to become professor of neurology, because the glass ceiling was still well and truly there. To prove herself, she'd already had to work twice as hard as the men in her field. Which meant making sacrifices. That meant no serious relationships—and no baby.

Though, holding Chloë in her arms and breathing in that sweet new-baby smell, for a brief second Vicky wondered if it was worth it.

Then she banished the doubt. Of course it was. It was what she'd always wanted to be, ever since she'd been tiny. To be a senior doctor and really make a difference. And she knew she couldn't have it all—so what was the point in wondering 'what if'?

'Vic?' Seb looked worried. 'Are you all right?'

'I'm fine.'

'No, you're not. You're working too hard. Vic, I know you want to be professor—and I also know you'll make it. But don't kill yourself in the process.'

'I'm fine,' Vicky repeated. 'Don't nag.'

'I could set Alyssa on you. Or Sophie. Or both.'

Vicky smiled. 'It won't work, Seb.' Her sisters-in-law were both doctors, too—Alyssa worked in emergency medicine and Sophie was a surgeon. 'They know the score.'

For a moment, she thought Seb was going to argue, then he gave a resigned sigh. 'All right. I'll shut up about that. So, will you?'

'What?'

'Be godmother.' Seb rolled his eyes. 'Hopeless. Ask you a question about neurosurgery and you'll talk for hours. Ask you about something social…'

'I'm not *that* much of a nerd. And, thank you, I'd be honoured to be godmother.' Vicky smiled. 'Especially as you named my very first niece after me.'

'If she has half your qualities, I'll be proud of her,' Seb said.

Vicky blinked. Was she hearing things? Had her brother—who normally teased her stupid—just paid her an incredible compliment? 'Marriage has definitely made you soppy.'

'No. I've realised what's important. And there's more to life than your job.'

Vicky had a nasty feeling she knew what was coming next. 'Don't you dare try to matchmake. I'm perfectly happy as I am. I stayed out of it with you and Charlie.'

'Liar. You arranged a fundraising raffle, offering a date with me as the prize to buy Charlie some time away from the paparazzi's attention so he could work things out with Sophie. And you as good as told Alyssa she had to marry me.'

'Don't listen to your daddy,' Vicky informed her niece. 'I didn't interfere at all. I just pointed a few things out and helped them see their way a little.'

'And I'm very glad you did,' Alyssa said, joining them in the living room. 'Has Seb asked you?'

'Yes. And I'm delighted to accept.'

'Good.' Alyssa smiled warmly at her. 'Though what I heard Seb saying is right. You *do* work too hard, Vic.'

'And I like being that way. End of discussion,' Vicky said. Though she was canny enough to go for the ultimate distraction, where new parents were concerned. 'Are Chloë's official photographs back, yet?'

To her relief, both Alyssa and Seb took the bait

and were soon clucking over their baby's first official photographs—and Vicky's personal life was left where she liked it best.

Ignored.

# CHAPTER ONE

JAKE walked quietly into the neurology department in the middle of the Wednesday morning—
the day before he was supposed to start. A bit
sneaky, perhaps, but he knew it was the best way
to see what his new department was *really* like.
When nobody was on their best behaviour, waiting for their new consultant to turn up.

Everything seemed fine. The department was
busy, but calm and quiet: clearly the team was
well established. The ward was clean and there
were gel dispensers by every bed: another good
sign. He'd worked in some truly horrible places
where the admin staff wasted money left, right
and centre and important things—like basic hy-
giene—suffered.

There was a board to say where the doctors and
senior nursing staff were, and another to show

who was looking after which patient, so communications were good, too. It was definitely a well-run department.

And then a woman stepped out in front of him. She was clearly a doctor, because she was wearing an open white coat and there was a hospital identity badge round her neck on a lanyard. Though she was the most gorgeous woman he'd ever set eyes on. Tall—nearly five feet ten, he'd guess, because in heels she could look him in the eye. Long, long legs, and her dark suit didn't hide the fact that she was all curves. Dark wavy hair, caught back at the nape of her neck. Slate-blue eyes. And the most kissable mouth he'd ever seen.

Every nerve in his body hummed. For a moment, he forgot where he was. Who he was. He just wanted to take that one step forward, pull her into his arms, loosen her hair, bend her back over his arm and kiss her. Just like in the movies.

'Can I help you? Are you looking for someone?'

The plummy accent shattered the dream and brought him back to reality. Sex goddesses didn't have silver spoons in their mouths, and this one was definitely posh—and rich, because on closer inspection that suit looked as if it was a designer cut. Plus, in his experience, doctors of that class who weren't working in private practice were usually just waiting in a cushy niche until something better came along.

Add the fact that she was just about to become his colleague, and that put her way off limits. On the rare times he did date, it was never another member of staff in his department. He'd seen first-hand what a mess it made at work when the relationship ended. Awkwardness at work, the headache of working out new rotas so the once-close couple were on opposite shift patterns… It just wasn't worth it.

Even if she was the first woman in a long time to make his skin tingle like that.

'Thank you, but I'm fine,' he said coolly.

Though he couldn't just pretend he'd wandered in off the street. He'd have to work with her—Dr Victoria Radley, according to her ID card—tomorrow, and playing games now would just make things awkward later on. Better tell the truth. 'I'm Jake Lewis.' He held out his hand.

'You're a day early.'

He felt the flush steal over his cheekbones, and was cross with himself for it. He was her senior, for goodness' sake. Why was he acting as if he were the naughty schoolboy and she was the head-mistress? 'I was passing, so I thought I'd drop in.'

Drop in? More like he was giving them the once-over before he started, Vicky thought.

Which was just what she would have done, in his shoes.

She took his hand and shook it briefly. Firm grip, dry palm—good. But there was something else. Something odd. Even though he wasn't touching her any more, she could still feel his skin against hers. And although it had been a business-like handshake, it had felt somehow intimate. Almost caressing.

She shook herself. How ridiculous. She never, ever had fantasies like this. Particularly about co-workers.

As consultants went, Jake Lewis was a little…different. Cheap suit, cheap shoes. Most of the ones she'd met were keen to show off their tailor-made clothing and hand-made Italian shoes. Maybe Jake Lewis wasn't interested in fashion; maybe, refreshingly, he was more interested in medicine.

Not that it should bother her either way. She'd already placed him neatly in his pigeonhole. The one marked 'C' for colleague. Not 'L'. *That* pigeonhole was nailed up, and she intended it to stay that way. No distractions.

She summoned up her professionalism. 'You've just missed a ward round. But I can round up the staff who are in if you'd like to meet them.'

'No, I'll leave it until tomorrow.'

Abrupt. Hmm. She just hoped his people skills were a bit better when it came to patients. Shame. If he smiled, he'd be very nice-looking. Tall enough to look her in the eye. Dark, soulful eyes. Dark hair that flopped over his forehead and was just a little too long at the back. And a mouth that made her want to reach out and touch…

Um, no. Apart from the fact that he was going to be her colleague in less than twenty-four hours' time—a senior colleague, at that—she didn't do this sort of thing. Work 1, Relationships 0. That was the score: the way it had always been and always would be, at least until she became a professor of neurology. Then she might reassess the situation. But absolutely not until then.

'Is there anything else you'd like to see?' Ugh. That sounded as if she was flirting with him. Which she wasn't. Gritting her teeth, she added, 'What I mean is, it might save time tomorrow if I show you where the staffroom is, the lockers and the kitchen.'

Anything else you'd like to see? Jake really was going to have to drag his mind out of the gutter. He just hoped he didn't have a dopey look on his face. Mind you, Victoria Radley was probably used to men falling at her feet. Any man with red blood in his veins would have a bad case of lust within seconds of meeting her. 'No, I'll leave it.' Basically because he couldn't trust himself. If he followed her, he'd be assessing the way she walked. Watching the curve of her bottom. Wanting to touch. Wanting to spin her round and kiss her. 'I just dropped by on impulse.'

The look on her face said she didn't believe a word of it.

'And I'm sure you've got things to do,' he added.

The amusement vanished from her face, and he realised what he'd said. He'd meant it as 'I don't want to take up your time', but she'd clearly taken it as 'You're slacking'. Hell.

Before he could explain, she said coolly, 'You're quite right. No doubt I'll see you tomorrow, Mr Lewis.'

And she turned on her heel and walked away.

Jake swore to himself. If he left it, she'd be all ice towards him tomorrow—and she'd probably tell her colleagues that the new boy was going to throw his weight around. If he chased after her and explained himself, he'd end up sounding like a gibbering idiot. Either way, he lost.

Well, icy professional was marginally better than fool. They'd soon find that he thawed out. So he'd take the lesser of the two evils. And he'd sort it out with Victoria Radley tomorrow.

# CHAPTER TWO

'I WONDER if Jake's single?' Gemma, the ward sister, asked.

Vicky shrugged. 'I'm more interested in whether he's good at his job.'

Gemma gave Vicky a searching look, which Vicky ignored. Honestly. When would her colleagues understand? She wasn't interested in having a relationship until she'd got where she wanted to be in her career. And she really wasn't interested in Jake Lewis, their new consultant. She was still annoyed with him about yesterday—she'd tried to make him feel welcome, and he'd made her feel as if she were slacking.

He'd find out his mistake soon enough. Victoria Charlotte Radley was far from being a slacker. And although part of her wanted to see him eat humble pie, the sensible part of her knew it was best to just ignore it and get on with her job. Emotions of any sort—except where her brothers and new niece were concerned—just weren't part of her life.

'He seems nice. And you have to admit, he's good-looking,' Gemma continued. 'Tall, dark and handsome to a T! And those eyes—they're really come-to-bed. Like melted chocolate.'

Vicky sighed inwardly. Either Gemma hadn't got the message or she didn't want to. Before Vicky had a chance to explain—firmly but politely—that she really couldn't care less if every other woman in the hospital thought Jake Lewis was sex on legs, because it really wasn't relevant, her pager bleeped.

She glanced at the display. 'I'm needed in ED. I'll finish the ward round later and I'll ring down when I know which theatre I'm in.'

'OK. I'll fill the board in for you,' Gemma said.

'Thank you.' Vicky smiled at her and headed for the emergency department.

'Dr Radley—you paged me,' she said to the receptionist.

'Yes—it's one of Hugh's patients. I'll just get him for you.' She returned with a doctor in tow.

'Hugh Francis, SHO. Thanks for coming, Dr Radley,' he said, smiling at her. 'I've got a ten-year-old with a suspected subdural haematoma.'

'Did he fall?' Vicky asked.

'Tripped up and hit his head on a skateboard ramp.'

Vicky frowned. 'Wasn't he wearing a helmet?'

'I couldn't get much out of him,' Hugh admitted. 'He was pretty scared. But he told Ruth—one of our staff nurses—that he's been having some problems with bullies. A gang of them waylaid him in the park this morning on the way to school, kept on and on about how useless he was and how he couldn't do some move or other on the skateboard ramp. They goaded him into trying it—but, of course, he didn't have a helmet with him and they said he was a coward if he didn't do it without.'

Vicky groaned. 'And he thought they'd lay off if he did what they wanted.'

'Something like that.'

But bullies never let up. If you proved yourself and did what they said you couldn't do, they'd find something else. On and on. Nag, nag, nag—until you finally snapped. And girls were probably worse than boys, because they went for mental torture. Being clever and being an Hon. had marked Vicky as a major target at school. She hadn't said a word to her mother, knowing that Mara had been too self-absorbed to do anything about it. But Charlie had found Vicky crying one afternoon after school and had made her tell him what was wrong. He and Seb had taught their younger sister the rudiments of judo so she could defend herself—and Vicky had practised on them enough to make sure that when she finally gave in to the demands for a cat-fight on the playing field, she'd left the bullies flat on their backs and crying. She'd had detention every lunchtime for half a term afterwards, but it had been worth it. The bullying had stopped.

'Poor kid,' she said feelingly. 'Was he knocked out, do you know?'

'He says not. But he was late for school, and the teacher picked up that he seemed a bit confused and drowsy. She wondered if he'd been sniffing glue or something and sent him to the first-aid room. He said he had a headache but wouldn't tell anyone anything.'

Of course not. If you told, it just drove the bullying underground. They were sweetness and light in front of the teachers, and when you were on your own you were really in for it. No more nasty letters, because they could be traced back—but there would be name-calling, deliberately breaking your things, accidentally-on-purpose tripping you up, or taking something precious and playing 'catch' with it until you were running frantically around like a hamster on a wheel, desperate to get it back.

She forced the memories back and stiffened her backbone. 'Lucky the first-aider sent him to us, then,' she said.

'She couldn't smell any substances. So she called his parents and told them to get him here, stat.'

'Good. What have you done so far?'

'GCS 11, pupils equal and reactive, ears OK.' Hugh frowned. 'But I'm not happy with his blood pressure, pulse or respirations.'

'Checked the eyes with an ophthalmoscope?' she asked.

'Yep. I think the intracranial pressure's rising, but I want a specialist's opinion.'

'OK. I'll take a look. I think a CT scan's a good idea—can you organise one?'

'Already booked.'

Vicky smiled. Just what she liked to see: a junior doctor who knew what he was doing and who had the confidence to act on his own initiative. If this was the way Hugh Francis usually worked, he'd be in the running for the next registrar's post in ED. 'Well done.' She walked with him to the cubicles. A pale, gangling boy was lying on the bed, and a worried-looking woman was sitting next to him.

'Mrs Foster, this is Dr Radley. She's a neurology specialist,' Hugh introduced her. 'Dr Radley, this is Declan.'

'Hello, Declan—Mrs Foster.' Vicky sat down on the side of Declan's bed and held the boy's hand. 'My name's Vicky, and I'm going to be looking after you for a bit. I hear you've had a bit of an argument with a skateboard ramp. I'm just going to have a look in your eyes, if that's all right with you, and then we're going to send you for a scan to see if there's anything making you feel rough.'

'I'm sorry,' he mumbled. 'Don't want to be any trouble.'

'Hey, that's what I'm here for.' She squeezed his hand. 'We'll sort it out, sweetheart.'

Hugh handed her the ophthalmoscope. She checked in Declan's eyes, and nodded. 'Yes, I definitely want to see a scan. Do you know what a CT scan is, Declan?'

'No.'

'It's a special sort of X-ray that takes pictures of your head from lots of different angles—it pictures slices inside your head. I'll show you them later on a computer, if you like—not many people get to see inside their own heads. And I might be able to arrange a film to be printed for you so you can show your mates later.'

'Haven't got any mates.'

It was said without any emotion, as if he didn't care, but Vicky would bet otherwise. She remembered that feeling herself, only too well. Being an outsider, the last person picked for a team, and trying to pretend to everyone else that it didn't matter…when it *did*. 'Do you go to an all-boys school?' she asked.

'No.'

Half her problems had stemmed from going to a single-sex school where she just hadn't fitted in. If she'd gone to a co-ed school, things might have been very different. 'Let me give you a little bit of advice,' she said softly. 'Try chatting to the girls.' Ten was an awkward age: boys still thought that girls were silly, and it was uncool to be seen talking to them. But what did Declan have to lose? Nothing but his loneliness. 'You might find some of them like the same things you do.'

'Girls don't like Game Boys,' Declan said. 'Or the Romans.'

'I liked computers when I was your age,' Vicky told him. 'So I reckon you might be in for a nice surprise. Give it a try. What have you got to lose?' She smiled at him. 'Now, Hugh here's going to take you off for a scan, and I'm going to have a chat with your mum.'

'Don't tell school,' Declan said. 'Don't tell them.' He nearly choked. 'Don't say what I told you. Please, don't.'

'It's OK,' Vicky soothed. 'There's nothing to worry about, I promise.'

Mrs Foster had clearly only just been holding it together, because a tear leaked down her face when Hugh wheeled Declan out. 'I'm sorry,' she said, wiping a hand across her face. 'I just feel so useless. I had no idea he was being bullied—what kind of parent does that make me?'

'A normal one,' Vicky reassured you. 'Believe me, it can be very hard to tell if kids are being bullied. Sometimes they go a bit quiet, sometimes they go the other way. But until they're ready to tell you, you won't know.' She'd done that herself. Kept it in, because she'd believed it was her fault and if anyone knew they'd despise her and treat her like dirt, too.

'Oh, God. I don't know what those little bastards have done to him. Or how long it's been going on—he won't say.'

'When you're bullied, you try to hide it—you don't want anyone knowing, in case the bullies get in trouble, because you're scared that then it'll get worse,' Vicky said gently. 'Or that somehow it's your fault, because you're different in some way—whether it's the way you talk, the colour of your hair, or you've got freckles. Whatever distinguishes you. But at least you know now, so you can help him. Keep his self-esteem high by praising him and making it specific so he knows you mean it and you're not just being nice, and maybe get him some martial arts lessons.'

'So he can hit back, you mean?'

'So he can defend himself against physical stuff,' Vicky corrected her dryly. 'Mrs Foster, I need to know a few things about Declan before I can do anything to treat him. Would you mind answering a few questions for me, please?'

Mrs Foster nodded. 'If I can.'

'Has he had any previous head injuries?'

'Not that I know of.'

Good. 'Is there any family history of easy bruising, or bleeding that doesn't stop?'

'No.'

Even better. 'Has Declan ever had a cerebral shunt?'

'What's one of those?' Mrs Foster asked.

'If he'd had hydrocephalus as a child, we would have operated to put a special valve in his head to drain off excess fluid—and it would have been replaced several times before now as he grew bigger,' Vicky explained. And Mrs Foster would definitely have known what a cerebral shunt was—the fact she'd asked meant it was highly unlikely Declan had had one.

Mrs Foster shook her head. 'No, nothing like that.'

'Does he have any allergies—penicillin or anything like that?'

'No. He's always been so healthy.'

Even so, Vicky needed to ask the last question. 'Is he taking any medication?'

'No. What's wrong with him?'

'I'll know more when I see the results of his scan, but I think he's got a subdural haematoma. That's a blood clot between the tissue of his brain and the membrane called the dura mater, which goes between his brain and his skull. It sometimes happens after someone bangs their head hard—the bridging veins between the brain and the membrane stretch and tear, a bit of blood leaks out and forms a clot.'

Mrs Foster's face turned a shade paler. 'Does that mean you'll have to operate?'

'I won't know until I see the scan,' Vicky answered honestly. 'Sometimes we can treat it without operating—just by careful monitoring—because smaller ones tend to go away on their own, but sometimes we need to operate before it puts too much pressure on the brain.'

'Oh, my baby,' Mrs Foster whispered.

'Is there anyone we can call for you?'

'M-my husband's on his way.'

'Good. If you want me to run through anything with you again, or you've got any questions, just let me know. That's what I'm here for.'

Mr Foster had arrived by the time Declan had had his scan. Vicky reviewed the files and pointed out one area to Hugh. 'I'm really not happy about this. I'm going to have to take him to Theatre.' She went back in to see Declan and his parents.

'Was the scan all right?' Mr Foster asked.

'I'm afraid not,' Vicky said gently. 'It showed me there's a clot forming between Declan's brain and the membrane covering it. It's pressing down on the brain and causing pressure, which makes the brain swell and not enough oxygen gets to it—that's why Declan's finding it a bit difficult to see and why he's sounding a bit confused. The good news is that I can operate—he'll have a general anaesthetic, and I'll cut a tiny lid into his skull so I can get the clot out. He'll need to be in here for about a week so we can keep an eye on him, but he should be fine.'

'Is he going to die?' Mrs Foster mouthed, turning her face away so Declan wouldn't see the question.

'There are risks, yes, but it's much safer to do the operation than to leave it,' Vicky said quietly. 'He'll have a headache afterwards, but he won't be in any real pain.'

'I'll kill them,' Mr Foster said between gritted teeth. 'I'll kill them for what they've done to our Declan. Just leave me on my own with them with a cricket bat.'

'Neil, no,' Mrs Foster said. 'You can't *do* that. That makes you as bad as they are.'

'Well, they're not going to get away with it,' Mr Foster declared.

'There are things you can do,' Vicky said quietly. 'But, right now, let's concentrate on getting Declan sorted.'

While Declan was being prepped for Theatre, Vicky rang up to the ward. 'I'm going to be in

Theatre Five.' And this was the bit she'd been dreading and looking forward to at the same time. 'Could you page Mr Lewis?' It didn't really matter whether she led or assisted: this was where she'd see what he was made of, and whether he was better with patients than he was with the staff. Or, at least, than he was with *her*.

She'd just scrubbed up when he came into the room. 'What have we got?'

'Craniotomy, to remove a subdural haematoma. The files are there, if you want to take a look.'

Jake reviewed the files swiftly. 'Good call. Have you done a craniotomy before?'

She nodded. 'I'd use a linear incision rather than the standard reverse question-mark incision in this case. We've pinpointed exactly where the haematoma is—and a linear incision will mean we spend less time controlling bleeding and it reduces surgery time.'

Jake's dark, dark eyes appraised her—and she thought she saw the glimmering of respect. But luckily she was prepared for his next comment. 'Good call. I'll lead, you assist.'

She'd told herself it didn't matter: but it did.

'How about I lead,' she said, 'and if you don't like the way I do it, you can take over?'

He finished scrubbing up before he answered her. 'All right. But you talk me through exactly what you're doing and why.'

Her mouth tightened behind her mask. 'Like a junior?'

'Like any other senior registrar on their first operation with a new consultant. It's a quick way of getting to know how we both work.'

Fair enough. He was still a bit abrupt for her liking, but maybe he'd discovered that she was the daughter of a baron and thought she was just playing at being a doctor. This was her chance to prove to him that she was serious—and she wasn't going to blow that chance.

As part of the preparation, Declan's head had been completely shaved. Instead of making him look like a thug, the haircut made him look like a defenceless little boy. Which was exactly what he was.

But there was no room for sentiment or emotion here in Theatre. Vicky had a job to do. And she was going to do it well.

'This is where I'm going to cut,' she said, indicating the area on Declan's head.

'OK,' Jake said.

Deftly, she cut through the layers of skin, muscle and membrane at the site. 'Burr-holes next,' she said, drilling a series of tiny holes. 'The bone's not too thick at this point, so I don't need to drill them very, very close together.'

She talked him through the rest of the operation—using a Gigli's saw, passed between the burr-holes using a malleable saw guide, then lifting the lid of bone back on a hinge of muscle so she could open the dura mater to reveal the inner membranes. 'Here's the clot. Suction and irrigation,' she said, working carefully to remove the clot. 'Here's the ruptured blood vessel. I'm going to clip it here.'

When she'd finished and was sure the blood vessel had stopped leaking, she gently replaced the bone, ready to sew the membranes, muscles and skin back into position.

'Want me to close?' Jake asked.

It wasn't really a question. He'd assessed her; now it was time for her to see how he worked. She nodded and stood back.

He was good. Fast, thorough and very deft. She'd never seen such neat stitching—and said so.

'Thank you.' He inclined his head slightly at the compliment, but didn't allow anything to detract from his focus.

That, Vicky thought, was impressive. She had a feeling she was going to enjoy working with Jake Lewis. A like mind, focused on his job. He really didn't care what people thought about him—the patient came first. Refreshing.

When they'd finished, he walked back to the ward with her. 'Do you want me to talk to his parents?'

She shook her head. 'I'll do it. They know me from the emergency department, and it's better that they have continuity of care as far as possible.'

'I agree. You know where I am if you need me.'

Meaning that he trusted her. Quite why that should make her feel enveloped in a warm glow, she had no idea. She already knew she did her job properly, so it shouldn't matter what he thought.

She went into the relatives' room, where the Fosters were waiting anxiously. 'I'm pleased to say the operation was a success. Declan should be coming round in a few minutes and you'll be able to see him straight away. We'll need to keep him flat for the next day or two so his brain can settle down again, and gradually we'll raise the head of the bed. We'll be assessing him very, very frequently and he'll have more CT scans over the next few days, so we can keep an eye on how he is and pick up on any little niggles before they turn into problems.' She decided not to mention the fact that the CT scan would pick up extra fluid; it was perfectly routine, but would sound scary to the Fosters and they were already upset enough.

'So he's going to be all right?' Mrs Foster asked.

'He should be,' Vicky said with a smile.

'Oh, thank God. Thank you.'

'And my consultant. If you have any questions, please, ask for me or Mr Lewis and we'll do our best to reassure you.'

'So that's everyone—oh, except Vicky, but you were with her in Theatre,' Gemma said.

'Dr Radley.'

Gemma grinned. 'Don't stand on ceremony. She doesn't even use her title around here.'

'Title?' That was news to Jake. What title?

'She's an Hon.—the Honourable Victoria Radley,' Gemma explained. 'Though she's always made it very clear she's a doctor first.' She smiled. 'You've probably heard of her brother, Charlie. Baron Radley.'

The name rang a bell, though Jake wasn't sure why. He never bothered with celebrity magazines or gossip pages in the paper.

'But don't go thinking she's a snob or anything like that. I mean, she doesn't tend to go on ward nights out, but it's not because she thinks she's too good for us. It's because she's writing a paper or she's got the chance to shadow someone on a particularly interesting case.' Gemma sighed. 'She works too hard.'

'Nothing wrong with being dedicated,' Jake said. He'd had that accusation thrown at him a few times, too. And if Vicky was dedicated, that explained why she'd been so confident during the craniotomy.

But an Hon....

It was only then that Jake realised he *had* been thinking about acting on his attraction to Vicky.

Asking her out for a drink, perhaps. He already knew she wasn't married so he didn't think he'd be treading on anyone's toes. But being an Honourable put her miles out of his league socially. Someone who was used to mixing with the likes of royalty wouldn't want to go out with a boy who'd grown up on a council estate.

Better to know now before he made a fool of himself. And that would teach him for thinking about breaking his personal rules. Vicky was a colleague, so she was off limits. For good.

# CHAPTER THREE

AFTER a fortnight at the Albert Memorial Hospital in Chelsea, Jake felt as if he'd been there for years. He'd been accepted as part of the team and he'd been included in invites to drinks to celebrate a staff nurse's twenty-fifth birthday, as well as the team night out at the local Indian restaurant. He'd gone to both and had had a great time—though he'd noted that Vicky hadn't been to either event. Technically, she'd been on duty, covering for other staff—but after a couple of glasses of wine Gemma had let it slip that Vicky always covered staff nights out. Vicky worked on bank holidays, Christmas and Easter, too, so staff with children could spend time with their families. And when she did take time off, she was booked onto a course or had arranged to shadow someone and get more experience.

And he still hadn't apologised to her, he remembered, feeling guilty. Not that he'd had the chance. She'd kept all conversation to a minimum, and what she'd said had focused entirely on their patients. But he didn't think she was a snob: her manner with patients was too good for that. So was she just avoiding him? And was that because he'd been rude to her the very first time they'd met—despite the fact he'd given her a genuine compliment on her surgical skills since?

He'd do something about it today, he decided, and did the last five reps on the lateral raise machine before leaving the weights room for the pool. Twenty lengths, and he'd hit the shower. Then a bacon sandwich and a strong, sweet cup of coffee in the staff canteen, and he'd be ready to start the day on the ward.

And he'd talk to Vicky. Today.

There were already three or four people in the pool. But only one of them arrested his attention. She was doing lengths—but the front crawl she used was a precise and neat stroke, rather than flashy. She looked as if she'd been trained professionally, to get the maximum speed from the minimum stroke, and her whole attention appeared to be focused on her swim. Up and down, up and down, face in the water, turned to the side for a breath between strokes, then straight again. Jake couldn't quite put his finger on it, but something about her drew him.

He dived cleanly into the pool when she was part way through a length. Surfaced beside her. And nearly forgot to swim when she turned her face towards him for a breath and he recognised her.

Victoria Radley.

Well, he shouldn't have been so surprised. Clearly she was as focused when doing exercise as she was at work. But one thought wouldn't go out of his head: *was she that focused when she made love?*

Oh, for goodness' sake. They were both professionals. She was his colleague. He wasn't supposed to be thinking about her in those terms. He didn't have room in his life for a relationship right now.

But the thought wouldn't go.

And when she climbed out of the pool—how on earth could she manage to look so elegant, scrambling out of the pool?—Jake found himself swimming straight for the side, ignoring the fact that he hadn't done the twenty lengths he'd promised himself, and also climbed out of the pool.

He fell into step with Vicky just before she reached the entrance to the changing rooms, and tried his best to sound casual. 'Hi.'

'Oh. Hello.' Cool, no flicker of friendliness.

'I didn't know you were a member here.'

She shrugged. 'It's the nearest gym to the hospital.'

Mmm, he'd worked that one out, too. And it meant no wasted time travelling to the gym—so he wouldn't have to get up at an unearthly hour or rush to the ward after a training session.

Her words were perfectly polite, but there was no hint of invitation in her voice. She was just the cool, calm professional he knew from the hospital.

And he wanted to know what lay beneath the smooth, unruffled mask. What made Victoria Radley tick? What made her smile? What made her eyes light up? What made her angry, and what made her laugh?

'Will you have breakfast with me?'

Those beautiful blue eyes widened. Clearly she hadn't expected that. He hadn't expected it either. His mouth had worked before his brain had gone into gear.

'I really ought to get to the ward,' she said.

'You're on the same shift as I am. Which doesn't start for...' he glanced at the clock '...forty minutes. We've got time for a shower and breakfast.'

There was the slightest, slightest flush against her cheekbones. And it vanished before he was really sure that she'd blushed. But he hadn't said anything out of place...had he?

Unless she'd interpreted 'shower' and 'breakfast' rather more intimately than he'd intended.

And that thought alone set his whole body tingling, as if champagne instead of blood was whooshing through his veins. He pulled himself back together with an effort. 'I hear the staff canteen does an excellent bacon sandwich,' he said.

And it'd be just his luck that she was vegetarian.

She said nothing.

Still sore at him? 'My shout,' he said, 'because I need to talk to you about something.'

That got a reaction. 'What?' She sounded suspicious and her eyes were slightly narrowed.

'Work.'

It was almost as if he'd waved a magic wand, because she seemed to relax again. 'OK. Meet you in the lobby in ten minutes?'

Most women he knew would take at least half an hour to get ready after a workout. But he was beginning to realise that the Hon. Victoria Radley wasn't like any other woman he'd met. 'Ten minutes,' he agreed.

And then she did something that threw him completely. She smiled. A *proper* smile. And his heart rate practically doubled.

He'd only just got his pulse back to normal when he reached the lobby, still slightly damp, nine minutes later. Precisely sixty seconds after that, Vicky joined him.

'I had a call from the hospital CEO yesterday,' he said as they walked down to the hospital.

'Oh?'

'About Declan Foster. His parents wrote in and said how good you'd been.'

Vicky shrugged. 'Just doing my job.'

'And a bit more besides. I've noticed your paperwork is meticulous and you always make sure that the patients, as well as their relatives, know exactly what's going on. And I think teaching a small boy to play chess might not be in your job description.'

'It was as good a way as any to spend a lunch-break,' Vicky said lightly.

'*Several* lunch-breaks,' he corrected. He'd noticed.

She frowned. 'Do you have a problem with that?'

'No, as long as you're not overdoing things. We all need time to recharge our batteries, Victoria.' At her sharp look, he added, 'May I call you Victoria? I prefer working on first-name terms.'

For a moment, he thought she was going to say no. Then she nodded. 'It's Vicky.'

'Vicky.' He could actually taste her name. Crisp, slightly astringent. And it made his mouth water.

Oh, he needed coffee. Before he said something stupid. 'You're supposed to take breaks.'

'I'm fine.'

There was a slight edge to her voice, and he sighed inwardly. 'I'm making a mess of this. What

I'm trying to say is, I'm sorry. When we first met…I didn't mean to imply you were a slacker. You caught me on the hop, doing a recce. I was embarrassed, and I said the first thing that came into my head.'

'I see.'

Clearly she wanted him to eat humble pie. OK. As long as it meant she kept talking to him, he'd do it. 'You're dedicated. Very dedicated. I've never met anyone who works this hard before.'

'It's the only way to break through the glass ceiling,' she said as they walked into the canteen.

The glass ceiling? That was something he hadn't even considered. 'This is the twenty-first century. It's supposed to mean equal opportunities.'

She raised an eyebrow. 'How many female heads of department do you know? How many women professors?'

He thought about it. 'Not many.'

'Exactly. If they have a family, they're expected to take a career break, which holds them back because they've spent five years raising children and need to brush up their skills again—not to mention the years of experience they've lost and the fact their male colleagues are now five years ahead of them. If they don't take a career break, they get a reputation as hard women who don't care enough about their families, and it's held against them.'

He frowned. 'Discrimination is illegal.'

'But it happens.'

He had no answer to that. 'So I take it you don't have children?'

'No.'

He just about managed to stop himself asking the next question. *And what does your partner do?* Because it was none of his business whether she was involved with someone or not. And he'd already told himself he wasn't going to act on his attraction to her. He needed to talk about something neutral. Fast. 'What would you like for breakfast?' he asked as they reached the canteen.

'Coffee, fruit and yoghurt, please.'

Polite and distant again. Which was what the professional in him had wanted—but what the man in him *hadn't* wanted. 'Do you mind if I have a bacon sandwich?'

She gave him a wry look. 'They're your arteries.'

When they sat down, he added tomato ketchup to his sandwich. 'Lycopene,' he said with a grin.

'Which doesn't negate all the cholesterol,' she shot back.

'Don't care.' He bit into the sandwich. 'Oh, *yes*. This is seriously good.' He nodded towards the half-sandwich on his plate. 'Sure you don't want to share?'

Vicky adored bacon sandwiches. Had it been Seb or Charlie opposite her, she wouldn't even have waited to be asked. But sharing a sandwich was *intimate*. She barely knew Jake—and it was going to stay that way. She couldn't afford a relationship. Not when she was so close to getting a consultant's post. If she let herself get distracted, her career would go straight down the plughole. She'd worked too hard, too long, to let that happen now. 'Quite sure, thank you.' She poured yoghurt over her fruit. 'So what did you want to talk to me about besides Declan?'

'I did the getting-to-know-you bit with the rest of the staff on team nights out.'

And because she'd been covering the ward, he

hadn't had the chance to have that kind of chat with her. She sighed. 'I'm sure my personnel file will tell you all you need to know about me.'

'That you're a senior registrar, that your exam results were superb, that your appraisals have always been excellent, and you're tipped for the next consultant's post.'

If he'd already reviewed her files, what else did he want to know?

The question must have shown on her face, because he said softly, 'I don't know *you*. I've seen how you are with patients and staff, and I'm impressed.'

Please, don't let him be trying to come on to her. She knew her willpower was strong, but she didn't need the extra temptation. Jake Lewis, with his dark eyes and the floppy hair that made him look like a disreputable cherub, could be a temptation. Like rich, dark chocolate. Addictive. 'You've reviewed my files and you've seen me work. That's all you need to know,' she said primly.

'Wrong. If I'm to develop the staff on my team—so they're happy in their jobs and work well for me—I need to know what they want out of their job. Where they want to be in five years' time, and what they think they need to get there. Where they think they're weak and need more experience or more training. Things that aren't written in files.'

Was he serious?

She risked a glance. He looked serious enough.

Though he also looked good enough to eat, with his hair still slightly damp from the shower. She thought of rich, dark chocolate again and suppressed a groan. Jake Lewis was dangerous. Someone she needed to avoid.

'So what do you want, Vicky?' he asked. 'To be head of department? Professor?'

'Both.'

He nodded. 'From what I've seen, you've got the skill and the dedication to make it.'

Was he trying to curry favour? No, he looked completely sincere. 'Thank you.'

'So your plan is?'

'Consultant next year. Then a part-teaching, part-practising post—I want to do the academic side and work on some research, but I like working with patients too much to give it up. Plus, theory's worth nothing if it's unworkable in a real-life situation.'

'And what experience do you think you need now?'

'More surgery.'

'Noted,' Jake said. 'When you're in Theatre with me, I'll try to give you the chance to lead as much as possible.'

'Thank you.'

'And let me have a list of the training courses you want to go on.'

'There's a small thing known as the departmental budget,' Vicky said.

'Which is why I'm not promising to send you on every course you want to go on. But when I know what everyone's skills are, and where there are training needs, I might be able to arrange interdepartmental training. Shadowing, mentoring, that sort of thing.'

'Provided our head of department agrees.'

'He'll agree,' Jake said softly. 'I can be very persuasive.'

Vicky looked at his mouth and thought, I just bet

you can. Then she stifled the idea. She was *not* going to start thinking about Jake Lewis in that way.

'And I find a cost-benefit analysis usually does the trick,' he added.

He understood admin as well as medicine? Interesting. In Vicky's experience, most doctors were either people-oriented or paper-oriented. They couldn't do both. That made Jake a rarity.

'Why did you become a doctor?' he asked conversationally, as he added sugar to his coffee.

'Because medicine was interesting.' And because it was a challenge.

'Anyone else in your family a doctor?'

Why did he want to know? It had no relevance to the way she did her job. 'My brothers,' she said shortly.

'Which specialty?'

That definitely wasn't relevant. And why did he want to know about her brothers? Charlie, with his rose-tinted glasses, would've said Jake was trying to be friendly. Seb—well, pre-fatherhood Seb—would've said Jake was a social climber, hoping that by making friends with her he'd get an introduction to the baron and invites to swish parties. Vicky was somewhere in the middle—and she wanted her brothers left out of this. 'Not neurology.'

She'd been short with him—rude, even—but he didn't have that you've-just-slapped-me-down look.

But before he could say anything else, her pager bleeped.

Perfect timing.

She glanced at the display. 'Thanks for breakfast. I'm needed in ED.'

'You're not on duty yet.' He frowned. 'Do you always have your pager switched on?'

'No.' Not always. Just ninety-odd per cent of the time.

His dark eyes held a hint of amusement, almost as if he didn't believe she'd been paged. As if he thought she'd called one of her friends from the changing room at the gym and asked them to bleep her in fifteen minutes' time—to get her out of a potentially difficult situation.

She'd thought about it, admittedly, but she also knew it would have fuelled gossip: why did Vicky Radley want to wriggle out of having breakfast with Jake Lewis? People would speculate. Rumours would start running round the hospital. So having breakfast with him had been the lesser of two evils. And it had been work-related, anyways. 'See you on the ward,' she said, and headed for the emergency department.

'Hello again,' Hugh Francis said with a smile when she reached ED. 'I was hoping it'd be you.'

'What's the problem?'

'Mrs Carter, seventy years old, suspected TIA—but I'm not sure if it's a very early stroke.'

'OK. I'll have a look. If I'm worried, I'll admit her to our ward.'

'Thanks.' Hugh took Vicky through to the cubicle where Violet Carter was sitting on the bed, and introduced her.

'I'm perfectly all right, you know. You don't need to fuss over me—you go and see someone who's *really* ill,' Mrs Carter said.

Vicky smiled at her. 'That's very public-spirited of you, but I'd like to check you over.'

'It was just a funny turn.'

'Tell me about it,' Vicky invited.

'It was like a curtain coming down over one eye. But it's gone now.'

Mrs Carter was describing a textbook case of amaurosis fugax, a typical symptom of a TIA or transient ischaemic attack, Vicky thought. 'Anything else?'

'I banged my knee when I answered the door, but that's just clumsiness. Old age.'

Or another symptom of a TIA. 'How about talking?'

'Perfectly normal. I think our postman's deaf, you know—he kept asking me to repeat things.' Mrs Carter sighed. 'I don't know why he insisted on bringing me here.'

Vicky glanced down at the notes. 'He was just worried about you. I think you might have had something called a transient ischaemic attack—called a TIA for short. It's where the supply of oxygen is cut off to part of your brain, usually by a blood clot. Your body can restore blood flow and break down any little clots, so that's why you feel perfectly all right now.'

'So I can go home?'

'Soon,' Vicky said. 'The thing is, if you've had

a TIA it means you're likely to be at risk of having a stroke in the future, so I want to check you over thoroughly before I let you escape. May I ask you a few questions?'

Mrs Carter nodded.

'Have you had a stroke before, or any recent surgery?'

'No.'

'Has anyone in your family ever had a seizure or a fit?'

'Not that I know of.'

'Have you had a virus or infection lately?'

'No.'

'Are you taking any medication?'

'I take water pills—the doctor says my blood pressure's too high—but I never forget to take them, because I've got one of those little boxes you put your week's supply in. My daughter got it for me.'

'And she lives near?'

Mrs Carter sighed. 'Yes. And she's a worrier, so don't you go telling her about this. I just stood up a bit too quickly when the postman rang, that was all.'

'Did you have any pain?'

'Not really.'

'Where was it?' Vicky asked.

'You're as bad as my daughter. She never gives up either,' Mrs Carter grumbled. 'Just a little bit in my chest. It's gone now. And, before you ask, I gave up smoking years ago and I eat proper meals. None of that microwave ready-meal junk.'

Vicky grinned. She could see herself being like Violet Carter in forty years' time. Dressed in purple and outrageously independent. 'Mrs Carter, I respect the fact you can look after yourself perfectly well. But I need to be sure you're not just being brave. If you do have any problems, I can give you medication for it and you'll be fine—but if you're not telling me something, you could end up being very ill.' When the old lady looked recalcitrant, she added her trump card. 'Which means I'd have to talk to your daughter, and she'd probably want you to live with her so she can keep an eye on you.'

'God forbid!' Mrs Carter exclaimed. 'I'd be up in front of the bench within a week.'

'The bench?'

'On a murder charge. I can't *bear* all that fussing. Not to mention putting up with teenagers slamming doors and listening to that rubbish they call music nowadays.'

'Me neither,' Vicky said feelingly. 'So is there anything you're not telling me?'

'I was a bit breathless. But I told you, I just stood up too quickly.'

'Would you let me examine you and run some tests, then?'

Violet rolled her eyes. 'If it means you won't tell my daughter, yes.'

Vicky smiled. From their discussion, she'd already been able to assess Violet Carter's attentiveness, ability to interact, language and memory skills—and they were all fine. But she checked the blood pressure in each of Violet's arms, then her respiratory rate and her temperature.

'I'm going to look into your eyes, if you don't mind.' She checked for retinal plaques and the pupils' reaction to light. Everything was fine.

Nerve testing was equally inconclusive. She started with the cranial nerves: there were no problems with Mrs Carter's eye movements and her eyelids closed normally; there were no problems with swallowing or the movement of her tongue; and the wrinkles on her forehead were symmetrical—no sign of drooping. Somatic motor testing told her a little more—there was no sign of tremor or any problems with the major joints or shoulder girdle, though there was a slight weakness on the left-hand side. When Vicky asked Mrs Carter to walk a few steps, her movements looked fine. She was able to put her finger on her nose and her heel to her knee.

'So are you satisfied I'm all right now?' Mrs Carter asked.

'Nearly. I'm going to send you for a CT scan—that's just so I can get a better look at what's happening inside your head.'

Mrs Carter snorted. 'If you could read my mind right now, young lady, I think you'd be shocked.'

Vicky laughed. 'No. I wish more people were as independent and determined as you are.' Mara certainly wasn't. Never had been, never would be, and Vicky was guiltily aware that too often she left Charlie to deal with their mother. Though so did Seb.

'As well as the CT scan, I'm sending you for an ECG—that's to check how your heart's working.'

'There's nothing wrong with my heart.'

'Good. But I'm still sending you for the tests. I want to know what caused you to have your "funny turn"—and I don't think it was anything to do with standing up too quickly. I'd like to make sure there isn't a clot hanging around that might give you a full-blown stroke or a heart attack.' At Mrs Carter's mutinous look, she added, 'Or I could just phone your daughter.'

Mrs Carter grimaced. 'You win. And I'd never play poker against you.'

'Chess is my game.'

'Never played it.'

'If your tests make me keep you in for observations, I'll teach you,' Vicky promised. 'And then you can extort promises from your grandchildren. If you beat them at chess, they have to turn the volume down and not slam doors.'

Mrs Carter gave her a narrow look, then grinned. 'You're on.'

'OK, Mrs Carter. I'll come and see you when your test results are in.'

'My name's Violet,' Mrs Carter said.

'Vicky.' Vicky held her hand out.

'I think you and I will rub along just fine,' Mrs Carter said, shaking her hand. 'You'll tell me the truth.'

'I will if you will.'

'And you'll keep my daughter out of it.'

'I'm not promising anything until I've seen your results,' Vicky warned. 'But if I can avoid worrying her, I will.'

'That's good enough for me.'

# CHAPTER FOUR

JAKE was in the middle of reviewing patient files ready for clinic when there was a knock on his door.

'Come in,' he called, and blinked in surprise when he saw Vicky. 'What can I do for you?'

'I'd like to discuss a patient with you.' She carried some films and a file with her. 'My ED case.'

So it *had* been a genuine case—not just a phone call from a friend she'd phoned earlier and asked to give her an excuse to get out of having breakfast with him. He'd wondered. And he was shocked at the rush of pleasure he felt now he knew it hadn't been an excuse. 'Sure.'

She quickly explained Violet Carter's case to him. 'From the symptoms, I thought it was a TIA. Carotid rather than vertebrobasilar. Anyways, the ECG shows I was right. There's carotid bruit.' Carotid bruit was a murmur over the carotid artery in the neck, showing that blood was having difficulty passing through the blood vessel.

'And?'

'I want to send her down to Radiology for magnetic resonance angiography to check the site of narrowing. If the stenosis is big enough, I'd recommend an endarterectomy.'

An endarterectomy was surgery to remove the lining of the arteries: a very delicate operation. Jake remembered what she'd said that morning about wanting more surgical experience. 'Have you done any before?'

'A couple by open surgery.'

'How about endoscopically?'

'No.'

'Right. Let me have a look at the MRA results. If we can do it endoscopically, I'll lead and you assist; if it's open surgery, you lead and I'll assist. If both sides are affected, maybe you can do one and I'll do the other.'

Vicky nodded. 'She's a nice woman, Jake. I like her. Feisty, independent—she's really going to hate the idea of being an inpatient.'

Yeah. Jake knew someone else like that. Except—

No. Now wasn't the time to think of Lily. Or wish he'd known back then what he knew now. If only he'd insisted… But he hadn't. He'd deferred to her wishes.

He couldn't change the past. Only the future— for someone else.

'Let me know when you've got the results. I'm in clinic for the rest of the morning.'

'OK.' She gave him an odd look. But he wasn't in the mood to find out why. He just wanted to see his patients and get his head back to where it ought to be before he met Violet Carter.

When Vicky reviewed the results, she sighed inwardly. Eighty per cent stenosis—the arteries were severely narrowed, which meant nowhere near enough blood was getting through them. This was definitely a case for operating.

She went to see Violet Carter. 'How are you doing?' she asked.

'Fine. Can I go home now?' Violet asked.

'No. I've found out what caused your funny turn this morning. Your carotid arteries are narrowed.' Gently, she ran her finger along one side of

Violet's neck. 'They run both sides of your neck and they supply the blood to your brain. If they become narrow, not enough blood or oxygen reaches your brain.'

'So what does that mean?'

'They're narrowed because some fatty material in your blood sticks to the lining of your arteries—it's called atherosclerosis. You have a choice. We can do an operation called an endarterectomy—what that does is remove the lining of the arteries and the stuff that's starting to block them, and the lining will grow back within a couple of weeks of surgery.'

As she'd expected, Violet caught on quickly. 'And if I don't have the operation?'

'They could block completely. Which means you'll have a full-blown stroke. If you want the figures, about half of people who have a TIA have a stroke within a year, and twenty per cent of those have a stroke within a month.'

'And if I have a stroke, I'll have to go into a home instead of being in my own place.'

Vicky nodded. 'You won't be able to look after yourself. You'll need care.'

'If I have the operation, I'll be all right.'

'There are no guarantees—but the odds are loaded in your favour.'

Violet seemed to be thinking about it. 'Would I be awake during the operation?'

'No, you'd have a general anaesthetic.'

Violet sighed. 'So I'm going to have to stay in.'

'For a few days,' Vicky explained.

'Which means I have to tell my daughter.'

'If you were my mum, I'd want to know,' Vicky said.

'Your mum's lucky,' Violet grumbled. 'She's got a sensible one who doesn't panic and run around like a headless chicken.'

Vicky's common sense was nothing to do with Mara. Besides, there wasn't room for two headless chickens in a family.

She pushed the thought away.

'I hope she appreciates you,' Violet said.

Vicky made a noncommittal sound. Mara didn't understand her and always said Vicky should have been born a boy. Especially after Vicky, as a five-year-old, had taken scissors to her tutu and ballet shoes and threatened to chop off her hair if anyone made her go back to ballet lessons.

Mara also hadn't appreciated Vicky getting herself expelled from finishing school in the first week. Or finding out that she could get herself made a ward of court so she could do her A-levels if Mara tried to make her go to another finishing school.

'I'll ring your daughter and explain the situation,' Vicky said. 'I can get you on this afternoon's list, if you'd like to sign the consent form.'

'And you'll be doing the operation?'

'With our consultant, Jake Lewis. I'll introduce you to him before the operation,' Vicky said. 'Oh, and in the meantime…' She pulled a magazine out of her pocket. 'Just to stop you getting bored.'

Violet took the puzzle book and flicked through it. 'Oh, *yes!* It's got those logic problems in it. I like them.' She smiled at Violet. 'Thank you, love. That's really kind of you.'

'Pleasure. I had a feeling you'd enjoy it.' Because Vicky could see herself like Violet, in forty years' time. Except she wouldn't have a daughter fussing over her, or teenage grandchildren. She just hoped a stranger would show her that same kindness.

\* \* \*

Vicky introduced Jake to Violet, and noted approvingly that Jake treated the elderly woman with respect, rather than talking down to her. He explained exactly what they were going to do and how long she'd need to be in afterwards, and that they were going to do the operation by keyhole surgery.

Though when they were scrubbing up, she noticed the brooding expression in his eyes.

'Are you all right?' she asked.

'Fine,' he said curtly.

Hmm. Maybe it was surgeon's nerves. Every surgeon she knew was keyed up before an operation—which was a good thing, as it meant they weren't taking their skills for granted and there was less chance of them being sloppy. Some people talked too much when they were nervous. Jake clearly went the other way and barely spoke at all.

Jake had chosen to operate to Corelli, surprising her. She'd expected him to work to pop music rather than classical. Then she was cross with herself for reacting in the same snobbish way Mara would have done. Sure, Jake had an East-End accent rather than a posh one, but since when did the way you spoke dictate your tastes in music?

He talked her through the two-hour operation, clearing one artery himself and then giving her a chance to work on the other carotid artery. She liked the way he worked: deft, neat, precise. But as soon as the operation was over he seemed to switch back to the brooding, uncommunicative man he'd been while scrubbing up.

Something was wrong. Not the operation—it had been a complete success. She didn't think it had been anything she'd done either. So had this op brought back bad memories? A patient he hadn't been able to save?

When Violet was out of the recovery room and had settled back on the ward—with her daughter fussing round her bedside—Vicky quietly slipped out to the canteen on her break. She bought a slice of carrot cake and two coffees—he took his black and sweet, she remembered—then headed for Jake's office and rapped on the door.

'Come in.'

He was doing paperwork at his desk, and there was strain in the lines of his face.

'What's this?' he asked when she closed the door behind her and put the coffee and cake on his desk.

'Carrot cake.'

Cake. The Hon. Victoria Radley had brought him cake. 'Why?'

She shrugged. 'The men in my life are cake addicts.'

Jake tried to squash the pinpricks of jealousy. He had no right to be jealous. She was a colleague—a distant colleague at that, barely even an acquaintance. *The men in my life…* He didn't think she meant that she had a string of men, but clearly she'd been good at keeping her relationships secret from the hospital grapevine. 'Oh.'

'Our cook made the best cake in the world,' she said, almost as if explaining. 'Which is why both my brothers are putty in the hands of any woman who gives them cake.'

Jake frowned. Was this her way of saying she wanted him to be putty in her hands? Or was she just explaining about the men in her life—her brothers?

As if in answer to his unspoken question, she said quietly, 'You looked upset earlier. I wanted to make you feel a bit better. It's also an apology for running out on you over breakfast this morning.'

He shrugged. 'No problem. You were paged.'

'Want to talk about it?' she asked.

Then he realised what was going on. Vicky had made a fuss over little Declan, who'd been bullied. She'd fussed over Violet, too, but on the old lady's terms—practical things, like bringing her a puzzle magazine. And now she was quietly adding *him* to her collection of lame ducks, bringing him cake and offering him a sympathetic ear.

'I'm fine,' he said stiffly.

'No, you're not. It's something to do with Violet.'

How did she know?

She must have been able to read his mind, because she said quietly, 'She got to me, too. I never really knew my grandparents because they died when I was very young. Violet's the kind I would've liked as a gran.' Her smile was suddenly bleak.

Jake knew exactly where she was coming from. The same place as him. Loss and loneliness. 'She reminds me of my nan,' he admitted.

'You were close to her?'

He nodded. 'She brought me up. My mum was a singer and Dad was her manager. They were always on the road, and Nan refused to let them drag me along with a home tutor or put me in boarding school. She said kids need a steady place to grow up.' He looked away. 'They were in America, flying interstate on my mum's first US tour, when their plane crashed.'

He was half expecting Vicky to trot out the usual platitudes or try to work out who his mum was, but she surprised him. 'Hard for you. How old were you?'

'Twelve.'

'That's a really tough age to lose your parents.'

Something in her voice made him look at her. The expression on her face...she knew exactly how it had felt. It had happened to one of her schoolfriends, probably. Another of her lame ducks.

'Yeah. But at least I had Nan.' Then, to his horror, the words he'd tried to bury whispered out of him. 'I just wish she'd seen me qualify.'

'Missed it by much?'

'Two terms.'

'Ouch. But, if it helps, she'd have known from your prelims that you'd qualify.'

At least Vicky hadn't gushed that his gran would have been proud of him. He appreciated that, because how did you ever know exactly how someone else felt—especially if you'd never met that person? That kind of reaction always drove him crazy.

Vicky Radley, on the other hand, was calm, practical and sensible.

He took a sip of his coffee to buy himself some time, and discovered that Vicky had sweetened it exactly to his taste. Which meant she was observant. He already knew she was clever, so she'd probably guess whatever he didn't tell her. So he may as well spill the rest of it. 'Nan died of a stroke. She had a TIA first, except she wouldn't admit there was anything wrong. It was only when our neighbour found her that she admitted she'd had a "funny turn". I rang home that night and got Bridget, who told me. I tried to get Nan to see her GP for a check-up at the very least. But she insisted it was nothing and I was making a fuss. Nan was one of the old school.'

'Stiff upper lip?'

'Sort of.' Though not posh, like Vicky's family. Lily Lewis had had backbone. 'She grew up in London during the Blitz. She hated being evacuated, so she ran away and made her way back to the East End. The way she saw it, if she managed to get through the war without being hit by a flying V, she wasn't going to let anything else throw her.' Including losing her only child. Lily had been the rock Jake had leaned on after the plane crash, and, even though her heart must have been breaking, she'd held it together for his sake. 'She'd just take the "funny turns" in her stride and pretend they hadn't happened.'

'TIAs.'

'Yeah. She wouldn't listen to me. And she ended up having a stroke.'

'So that's why you specialised in neurology?' she guessed.

He didn't want to answer that, though he guessed that the muscle he felt tightening in his jaw would give him away. 'If you hadn't persuaded Violet to let us do the endarterectomy, I'd have told her about my nan.'

'Bullied her into having it done?'

'Guilt-tripped her into it,' Jake corrected. Then he saw a flicker of a grin on Vicky's face. 'What?'

'Beat you to it. I told her the stats and let her work it out for herself: she could have it done and go back to her own home, or risk a stroke and being stuck in a care home. Or—worse, in her view—being fussed over in her daughter's home.'

'You understand your patients well.' With a flash of intuition, Jake guessed, 'You're the same, aren't you? You hate being fussed over.'

She nodded. 'Worst nightmare. Comes of being the youngest of three—and the only girl.'

'I remember you told me your brothers are both doctors. What are their fields?'

'Plastics and ED. And they insist on referring to me as "our baby sister, the brain surgeon".'

Teasing, but he'd guess that they were proud of her. And that they knew exactly what she was like: if they made a fuss over her and told her how they felt, she'd shut them out. So they teased her instead, saying the words in the way they knew she'd accept them.

Her family. People who loved her. Jake forced the surge of envy down. He'd made his decision years ago. Losing one family—his parents—had hurt enough. Losing his second, his nan, had been even harder. And he wasn't going to risk it a third time. He'd go out with the crowd, sure. But he wasn't letting anyone close. Wasn't going to have another family that he could lose.

And that included Vicky Radley. Despite the fact that his whole body yearned to touch her, hold her, he wasn't going to take the risk.

Asking her to breakfast this morning had been a mistake. He'd been listening to his libido instead of his common sense. Well, he wasn't going to make that mistake again. 'Thanks for the coffee and cake,' he said, though he hadn't touched a crumb. 'See you later.'

'Sure.'

To his relief, she took the hint and left his office.

Though he could still feel her presence in the room after she'd left. Still smell her perfume. And it made him ache for her.

An ache he dared not let himself soothe.

# CHAPTER FIVE

A MONTH they'd been working together. Four short weeks. And Vicky couldn't get Jake out of her head. Worst of all, she'd gone to Chloë's christening, had had a cuddle with her goddaughter at the party afterwards and had had this weird almost-vision of holding another baby.

A baby with huge brown eyes, just like her daddy's.

This was bad. Really bad. Vicky never, but *never*, fantasised like that. She didn't want children and she didn't want a life partner. She wanted a career. She wanted to blaze a trail in medicine and discover new things. She wanted to save people.

So why couldn't she get his face out of her head?

It was worse because she'd seen him practically naked at the pool. Jake's swimming shorts were perfectly demure, but she'd seen him dive into the pool at the gym they both went to. She'd seen his perfect musculature, the light sprinkling of hair on his chest, his strong, sturdy body. And she'd wanted to touch—something that had sent her straight to the side of the pool and out to the showers before she'd done something stupid. Like suggesting breakfast together. And not after a session at the gym, either.

She really had to do something about it. Sooner rather than later.

She sealed the envelope, addressed it and wrote PERSONAL on the front so Jake's secretary wouldn't open it, then slipped into Jake's office and put it in his in-tray.

Jake stood at the top of the Canary Wharf tower. He'd done this before, and he knew it was safe— he had a harness on and protective clothing—but adrenalin was still fizzing through him. In a couple of minutes he'd be walking backwards off one of the tallest buildings in London. Abseiling his way down.

And the ward had come up trumps. Everyone

had signed his sponsor form, from the auxiliary staff through to the director of Neurology, even though the money wasn't going to benefit their hospital.

Maybe the name had tipped them off. The Lily Lewis Unit. Named in honour of his grandmother—even though they hadn't been able to save her—because of the amount of money Jake had raised in her memory. Money that had bought vital equipment for the unit. Money that had saved people, the way he hadn't been able to save his grandmother.

He'd jumped out of planes—twice, once for his mum and once for his dad—and swum the equivalent of the English Channel. He'd abseiled down several buildings in London. Bungee-jumped from a bridge in New Zealand. Run marathons.

He couldn't think of a better way of using his spare time.

'This one's for you, Nan,' he whispered, as he stepped backwards into space.

And he ignored the fact that it was a pair of slate-blue eyes in his mind, not his grandmother's twinkling brown ones.

* * *

The following morning, Jake was going through his in-tray when he found an envelope. Handwriting he didn't recognise. Marked PERSONAL.

Odd. He slit the top of the envelope and shook out the contents. It was a cheque—a *large* cheque—from the account of V. C. Radley, made payable to the Lily Lewis Unit.

What on earth…?

He looked in the envelope again, but there was no note. Just the cheque.

Minimum fuss, like Vicky herself.

But she'd already signed his sponsorship form, given him a similar donation to those of the other senior staff. This didn't add up.

He slipped the cheque back into the envelope, put it in his jacket pocket, then went in search of her on the ward. 'Sorry for interrupting,' he said quietly to the patient she was talking to. 'Dr Radley, could I have a word in my office when you're free?'

'Of course, Mr Lewis.' Polite and neutral, just like he'd sounded.

Though inside he was fizzing. Just seeing her face drove his pulse up several notches. Oh, this was bad. He didn't do relationships. He was focused on his career and on fundraising. He didn't have space in his life for anybody. Especially someone who was so far out of his social league, she may as well be from another planet.

He forced himself to go steadily through his paperwork, but he found himself looking at the clock every few seconds. And it was another twenty minutes before she knocked on his office door.

'Take a seat,' he said, gesturing to the chair in front of his desk.

'What's the problem?' she asked as she sat down.

'You've already given me a cash donation. Why this?' He took the envelope from his jacket and waved it at her.

She shrugged. 'Why not?'

'Vicky, that's an awful lot of money.'

She was silent for a moment. Then she sighed. 'The grapevine must have told you by now about my family.'

'Well, yes,' he admitted.

'My father was a baron.'

*Was,* he noted. Past tense. So their discussion a

few days ago… Maybe she'd been sympathetic because she'd been there herself, not just supported a friend through it.

'I inherited money from the estate when I was much, much younger—money that my trustees invested in property. Which means I don't have a mortgage, and as a senior registrar I'm on a decent salary.' She stood up again and pushed her chair back. 'So it's not the big gesture you think it is. I can afford it. And I'd rather give the money to a good cause that will make a real difference to someone's life than waste it going clubbing and ordering bottles of overpriced champagne to rack up the profits of some sleazy barman.'

Any second now she was going to walk through that door and things between them would be awkward to the point of screaming. He was making a real mess of this. 'I'm sorry,' he said quickly. 'I meant to say thank you—and I wanted to say it quietly and without embarrassing you, the same way you gave me this cheque. But I'm a bit overwhelmed. People don't usually give me donations this big—not unless they've lost someone, too.' Was that it? Had her father

died from a stroke, which was why she'd specialised in neurology?

She didn't meet his eye. 'Consider your thanks
accepted.'

'Vicky.' He couldn't leave it like this between
them. 'Can I take you out to dinner?'

'No need.'

She thought he was trying to come on to her.
Well, he was. And he wasn't. 'I meant, in friend-
ship. As a way of saying thank you for your support. I'm not trying to talk you into a date.' Ha. Not
much. He hadn't been able stop thinking about her
since he'd met her, and he was getting close to the
point of breaking all his personal rules and asking her out for real.

'I'd rather you took the money you'd spend on
a meal and added it to the fund.'

OK. So she didn't want dinner. She was probably used to being wined and dined in all the best
restaurants in London. Places where you had to
have a name to get a table, or book up about a year
in advance. Places where dinner for two would
cost a week's wages for the average person.

So maybe he should offer her something different. 'OK. How about next time we both have a day off, you let me take you somewhere out of London?'

'Where?'

Vicky nearly clapped her hand over her mouth in horror. The word she'd meant to say was 'no'. 'Where' was tantamount to saying 'yes'.

'Come with me and you'll find out.'

Tempting. Too, too tempting. Just as she was about to grab her self-control with both hands and throttle it into submission, he added, 'As a friend.'

A friend? She'd never actually had a male friend. Except Seb and Charlie, and they didn't count because they were her brothers.

'Please?'

The word—coupled with the look in those deep, dark eyes—undid her. 'OK.'

He smiled. 'Good. By the way, you'll need to wear jeans and trainers.'

Hmm. She had running shoes, the ones she used at the gym. But jeans… She never wore jeans. Always suits. 'Why?'

'You'll see when we get there. So shall we synchronise off-duty?'

That sounded so cool and professional, it couldn't possibly be a date. Vicky relaxed and took her PDA from the pocket of her white coat. 'Fine.'

'Next Wednesday?' Jake suggested.

This was too close to a date for her comfort, but she swallowed the panic. He hadn't meant it as a date. 'I can do that.'

'Pick you up at your place?'

Her hesitation must have tipped him off, because he added, 'Not because I'm going to stalk you. But because it'll be quicker.'

'All right.' She gave him her address.

'Ten o'clock. So the rush hour is over.'

'Ten o'clock.' She typed 'JL' next to the date and time in her PDA. 'I have a ward round to finish, unless there was anything else?'

'No. See you later, then.'

Vicky made a noncommittal noise, and left his office.

Several times over the next three days she was tempted to cancel the arrangement. Except it wasn't a date...was it? All the same, she bought a pair of jeans. And at three minutes to ten on Wednesday morning she was leaning against the window-sill of her living room, which overlooked the road. Ninety seconds or so later, she saw a small red car pull into the parking space nearest to the gate, and Jake climbed out.

She'd seen him in a suit at work. She'd seen him in his swimming gear. But she wasn't prepared for the sight of Jake in a pair of faded denims, a crew-necked black sweater and sunglasses. He looked positively edible, and she had to take six deep breaths before she was able to answer her door and maintain her façade of being cool and profes-sional.

He gave her a long, appraising look, then nod-ded in approval. 'You'll do.'

It was one of those bright, warm April days, so she didn't bother with a coat. She made sure her door was double-locked, then followed him to his car.

He wasn't playing classical music on the stereo, she noticed. So maybe that bit in Theatre had been a pose, something to impress.

As if he guessed what she was thinking, he said, 'This is what I drive to rather than work to.'

'Who is it?'

'Keith Urban. Aussie country rock.'

She'd never heard of him. 'It's nice.'

For a moment, she thought she saw him grin. Amused, because she was being so polite. She *hated* people laughing at her. She folded her arms. 'So where are we going?'

'You'll see when we get there. Sit back and relax,' he advised.

There was nothing else she could do. Obviously, he knew exactly where he was going, so he didn't need her to navigate. Sitting doing nothing made her uncomfortable—she never lazed around like this—but she hadn't thought to bring a journal with her.

That was when she realised she'd expected him to make conversation. Except he didn't. He just drove and hummed along to the CD. In some respects, that was good: there was no pressure to be polite. But Vicky grew more and more keyed up, trying to work out where they were going. It wasn't immediately obvious from the signposts; the M25 circled London so it could lead to just about anywhere. But when they turned off onto the A127… 'Southend? We're going to the sea-side?'

'It's the nearest coast to London,' he said.

The seaside. Vicky couldn't ever remember going to the seaside as a child. They'd always had a week skiing at Klosters in the spring, then a week in Derbyshire with some distant relatives where her father had taken the boys climbing and Vicky had been stuck tagging along with Mara and a bunch of girls who'd liked dressing up and had regarded her as weird. That had been when Vicky had discovered a book of card games and had taught herself poker—then had fleeced her brothers of their pocket money until they'd agreed to make their father take her climbing, too.

After their father died, they hadn't gone skiing any more. She hadn't had the heart for it. And the idea of going on holiday with Barry, Mara's husband, hadn't borne thinking about. She'd used studying as an excuse to get out of family holidays, and the habit had stuck.

'Don't look so worried. You might even enjoy it,' he said softly as he parked the car.

'Sorry. I don't usually spend my days off like this.'

'You spend them studying.' He smiled at her. 'Well, today you're playing hookey. Recharging your batteries. And you'll be so relaxed that you'll catch up with your studies in record time tonight.'

She followed him out of the car. The seaside. The sound of the wind whipping the water into froth. Seagulls shrieking. Maybe it was the school holidays or something, because there were children on the beach, making sandcastles.

Vicky had never made a sandcastle.

Almost as if Jake had read her mind, he dived into the nearest shop and came out with two buckets and two spades.

She frowned. 'What are those for?'

'Challenge. Loser buys lunch.'

'What sort of challenge?'

He grinned. 'Biggest sandcastle wins.'

She knew the theory, but practice was another matter. She hadn't played with sand since nursery school. Her first bucketful of sand was fine. The second was missing a corner, and the third collapsed completely. And somehow Jake was already on the second storey of his castle.

He must have seen the dismay on her face, because he stopped. 'Change of rules. We're working as a team.'

'It's OK.' This was the sort of thing Jake ought to be doing with his kids, not with her. Not that he had any kids—well, to her knowledge. But he was clearly the sort of man who wanted children, wanted a family. Unlike her. She wanted her career. First, last and always.

'I have an unfair advantage, because I spent two weeks at the seaside every year,' he said. 'Nan used to find us a bed and breakfast somewhere on the east coast, usually wherever Mum had a summer season booked. I used to sit backstage while Mum sang at night, but we used to spend the days together on the beach, making sandcastles and looking for shells and poking around in rock pools and skipping stones. I even found some fossils when we went to Whitby one year. I found some jet, too.'

Simple, childish pleasures. Vicky had never had that. Her father had always been too busy with the estate—and when he hadn't, he'd tended to concentrate on Charlie. Mara had only wanted to do girly things—things that had bored Vicky rigid—so she'd found a hidey-hole in the attic at Weston where she could read. All she'd needed had been her torch, a glass of milk and the doorstep sandwiches Cook had wrapped in greaseproof paper and smuggled up to her.

'Sounds like fun.' She strove to keep the wistfulness from her voice.

'It was. We didn't have much money after my parents died, but Nan always saved up for our holiday. She said there's something about the sea air that blows your troubles away.'

'I don't have any troubles.'

He could see that. 'I guessed this one really wrong.'

'How do you mean?'

He'd made a mess of it. May as well finish it with honesty. 'You didn't strike me as the sort who ever went to the seaside. I wanted to give you a day with a difference.'

'It was a nice thought.'

'And so far you've hated every second of it.' All he'd done had been to deepen the gulf between them. Of course the daughter of a baron wouldn't do English seaside resorts—she'd do Monte Carlo or St Tropez. She wouldn't eat fish and chips straight from the paper, or lick sugar from her fingers after scoffing doughnut rings, or dangle a fishing rod over the end of the pier. She'd eat caviar and lobster thermidor and elegant puddings with spun-sugar decorations. 'Come on. I'll drive you back to London.'

To his surprise, she said, 'No. Show me what normal people do at the seaside.'

He stared at her. 'Normal?'

'People who don't have to watch what they do or say in case a reporter or a photographer is nearby.'

He hadn't thought of that. 'You mean, you get followed by the paparazzi? They're here?'

She shook her head. 'They don't usually bother with me. Charlie's the baron, so he gets most of it. And Seb used to be the darling of the gossip rags, because he was out partying all the time and never dated the same woman twice. But now they're both married and respectable.'

'But you're their sister. Why aren't the paparazzi after you?'

'Because there's no story in someone who just works and studies.'

Was that why she was so driven? As a way of hiding from the spotlight? 'Aren't you ever tempted to—I dunno—rebel? Do something outrageous?'

'No. I did that when I was little.'

Something in her eyes made him wonder. *'How* little?'

'Five.'

'You ran away?' he guessed.

She shook her head. 'Cut up my tutu and ballet slippers. And I told my mother if she made me go back to ballet class—or if she put rags in my hair once more, to give me ringlets—I'd cut off all my hair. I'd already done my fringe so she'd know I was serious.'

Jake chuckled. 'Wow. You were scary even then.'

'I'm not scary.'

She sounded offended. He winced. 'Um. Not with patients. But the standards you set…the rest of us have a hard time keeping up.'

'Your problem, not mine.'

And now she was back to freezing him. 'Vicky, I didn't mean it as an insult. I admire your strength of character.' He admired a few other things about her, too, but he didn't dare tell her that right now. 'Can we rewind?'

'Rewind?'

'Back to the bit where you asked me to show you what I used to do at the seaside.'

She was silent for so long that Jake thought she was going to say no. And then she nodded. 'OK.'

He gave their buckets and spades to the nearest family, then ushered Vicky over to the pier. 'This is the longest pleasure pier in the world—it's just over a mile and a quarter long and the water at the end is a mile and a quarter deep. Want to walk to the end or take the railway?'

'Walking's better for you.'

'But the train's more fun.'

'Compromise. Train there, walk back?'

He grinned. Just as he'd hoped, she was beginning to get the idea. This was meant to be fun.

They tried their hand at fishing at the end of the pier, and he bought her a dish of cockles.

'I'm not sure about this,' Vicky said.

'Fish is good for you. You're a neurologist. You should know what omega-3 oils do for you.'

'From oily fish, such as salmon. These—'

'Are what everyone eats at the seaside.' Jake splashed vinegar over his. 'They're fished locally, about five miles down the road at Leigh. It's an ancient cockle-fishing village.'

'Right…' She stabbed one with a cocktail stick, closed her eyes and put it into her mouth. She chewed once, twice and pulled a face as if she was barely able to swallow the tiny shellfish. 'Um, Jake, please, don't take this the wrong way…'

'You hate them.' He took the dish from her and made short work of it. 'I promise, you'll like the next thing.'

'Hmm.'

'You will. Southend sells the best ice cream in the world.' He shepherded her over to another kiosk, and bought her an ice cream cone with a chocolate flake.

'I don't think I've ever seen ice cream this white.'

'Trust me,' Jake said.

She gave him a sidelong look. 'After the cockles?'

'Just take a mouthful.' He ate his own with relish—and was delighted to see that Vicky enjoyed hers just as much. Though he decided not to push her into admitting it—he didn't want her to put her barriers up again.

She had the faintest moustache of ice cream. Jake was sorely tempted to lick it off himself, but he kept himself under control—just—and rubbed his thumb lightly over her lips instead. Every single nerve-end in his skin tingled at the touch.

Her eyes widened. 'What was that for?'

He showed her the white coating on his thumb. 'Ice cream.'

Lord, her eyes were beautiful. And they widened even more when he licked the ice cream off his thumb—ice cream that had been touching her mouth only seconds before.

He bought her fish and chips at the other end of the pier; they ate them straight from the wrapper, sitting on the beach. For just a moment the Honourable Vicky Radley looked like any other woman enjoying a day out with her man...

Except he wasn't her man.

Wasn't likely to be.

Neither of them had space in their life for a relationship.

He reminded himself that he was meant to be showing her what he used to do at the seaside, and dragged her into one of the amusement arcades. He won the first two games of air hockey, but she was a fast learner and beat him hollow in the third. They lost on the Camel Derby. Won a potful of pennies on the cake-walk cascade slot machine. And then they came to the soft toy 'grabber' machines.

'Which one do you want me to win for you?' he asked.

Vicky scoffed. 'Come off it. I've been watching other people. Those grappling hooks are meant to drop the toy just before it reaches the escape chute.'

'Which one do you want me to win for you?' Jake repeated.

'The teddy with the "kiss me quick" hat,' she said.

'And you'll call it Fred?'

She looked puzzled. 'Why Fred?'

He rolled his eyes. 'Because everyone needs a ted called Fred.'

'OK. *If* you win.'

He was almost tempted to suggest a side bet. If he won the teddy, she had to give him a kiss. But that would be unfair. Cheating, even. Besides, he didn't want to kiss her.

Much.

He put the money into the slot. Enough for five tries. On the first try, the grabber caught the bear's foot and lifted it a couple of centimetres before dropping it again.

'See? These things are meant to make money,' she said. 'If it was that easy, each go would cost a lot more—to cover the cost of the bear and the overheads and still make a profit.'

Oh, she could gloat. But he'd be having the last laugh. It had been years since he'd done this, but he was pretty sure he hadn't lost the knack.

His second try was just as much a failure. So was his third—and fourth.

'Last go,' Vicky said. 'Talk about hopeless.'

'I'm a brain surgeon. I operate with precision,' Jake said.

'In a theatre, yes.'

Right, that was it. 'If I win this time, you have to give me a kiss,' Jake said.

'Sure.' She was clearly enjoying the moment, expecting him to lose.

Jake hit the button, manoeuvred the grabber so that it caught the bear's middle, and it dropped neatly into the escape hatch.

He reached in, took the bear and presented it to her. 'Vicky, meet Fred.'

Her smile faded. 'You did it.'

'I told you, I went to the seaside for a fortnight every year. And there's a knack to doing this. Just like theatre. You just need to know how it's done.'

Oh, Lord. She hadn't bargained on that. And she'd been so confident he wouldn't do it—so sure, after she'd watched other people try their luck on the machines and lose—that she'd promised him a kiss.

She never broke her promises.

Which meant she had to kiss him.

His mouth really was beautiful. Tempting. She remembered how he'd wiped the ice cream from her lips and how she'd wanted him to kiss the mixture from her mouth instead. And now was her chance. All she had to do was lean forward and touch her lips to his. See where it took them.

He didn't look as if he was gloating. On the contrary, he looked as if all the breath had been sucked out of his body. Just how she felt. As if every nerve was tingling.

A kiss.

One little kiss.

A kiss that could change her entire life.

# CHAPTER SIX

VICKY leaned forward, kissed Jake swiftly on the cheek, and ducked away again.

He didn't say a word. He didn't have to: it was written all over his face.

*Coward.*

Wrong. Vicky wasn't a coward. She was practical. And this was self-preservation at its most practical. She needed distance between them—otherwise, she'd be tempted to kiss him properly. 'Thank you for the bear,' she said politely.

'Pleasure,' he said, his voice equally formal. 'Time for a doughnut, I think.' He shepherded her over to another kiosk, and bought a bag of hot sugary doughnuts to share.

Vicky—who'd noticed just how dark the oil was when she'd watched the little circles of batter floating on top and puffing out as they'd cooked—

really wasn't keen to taste one. But Jake was trying so hard to give her a good day out: how could
she rebuff him? Gingerly, she bit into one—and
was surprised at how good it tasted.

Maybe it was the sugar rush, but the awkwardness of the kiss-that-should-have-been had dis-
solved by the time they'd finished the doughnuts.

'Time for some beachcombing,' Jake said deci-
sively. She followed him onto the sand, and
watched as he stooped to pick up some shells.

'I spent hours doing this as a kid,' he told her. 'I
was always convinced I'd find a pearl in one of
these shells—if I found one with an orange band on
the end it meant there might be a pearl in it.' He
grinned. 'It was years before I worked out they
were cockleshells, not oyster shells, so I'd never
find a pearl. But I still collected them for the garden.'

'The garden?'

He nodded. 'We always came home from the
seaside with a huge bucketful of shells, and I'd
spend ages arranging them on the edge of the
flower-beds in our garden at home. You know,
like the nursery rhyme.'

Something else Vicky had never done as a child. They'd had enormous gardens at Weston, but Preece, the head gardener, had shooed her away if she or her brothers had gone anywhere near his beloved flower-beds. They'd all been told off for climbing the trees, too. And for playing hide-and-seek in the ancient yew hedges that made up the maze—it had been fun, wandering around the twisted branches and roots and pretending they were in the belly of a whale or a dinosaur, but Preece hadn't seen it that way. He'd just seen holes in his precious hedges and had gone straight to their father. Shortly afterwards, the maze had become out of bounds.

The more Vicky thought about her privileged childhood, the more she thought it had been a prison. Something that normal children were lucky to have escaped. Yes, Jake had lost his parents at a young age, and his mother's career had meant his parents had spent a lot of time away from him—but he'd grown up in a family where he'd been loved, allowed to explore and allowed to get his hands dirty.

On impulse, she slipped one of the shells into

the pocket of her jeans. She'd keep one. Just one. To remind her of today, the day she'd discovered what her childhood should have been like.

'There used to be an amazing fair here when I was a kid,' Jake said. 'I can remember this ride where you were all strapped to the inside of a drum, and when you were spinning at top speed the floor went down—but you were spinning so fast, you were stuck to the side of the walls and you stayed there until the end of the ride when the floor came up again.'

Funfairs. Something else she'd never done. Some of the wistfulness must have shown on her face, because he said softly, 'It's all changed here now—the rides are for kids, and anyways that kind of ride would breach all kinds of safety regulations nowadays.'

She nodded. 'Did you go to the funfair a lot?'

'Not as much as I would've liked to.' He shrugged. 'Nan saved all year for our holiday, and I saved the money from my paper round, but we didn't have much to spare.'

Whereas her family had had the money, but not the inclination. Her father would have dismissed the funfair as a waste of time, and her mother… Well, funfairs and candy floss didn't go with perfect manicures, designer outfits and expensive hairdos.

'But you don't need to spend a fortune to have fun. We used to poke about in the rock pools, and in the evening if Mum had a night off we'd sit on the cliffs with our fish and chips and watch the sun setting—not that it ever sets properly over the sea on the east coast,' he added, his eyes crinkling at the corners. 'Except at Hunstanton, in Norfolk—it's the only east coast resort that actually faces west.'

Such a simple thing: watching the sun setting and the moon rising. It triggered a memory, an image that had delighted her when she'd been younger. 'I remember reading this book when I was a teenager.' A romance novel she'd borrowed from their cook and read in her attic hidey-hole. 'It was set somewhere in Australia or New Zealand, I think, and when the moon rose it looked as if stairs were coming out of the sea and there were people dancing in the moonlight.' And she'd loved the idea of it.

'Stairs out of the sea in the moonlight?' He looked intrigued. 'We won't get *that* at Southend—

and it'll be about another five hours until the moon's out—but we can do the dancing bit.'

Before she'd quite grasped his intention, he'd spun her into his arms.

'You're quite safe. Fred's chaperoning us,' he said, nodding at the bear.

And then he was waltzing with her on the sand. Humming 'Moon River'.

She closed her eyes, and suddenly it was no longer a late afternoon in April on the English coast. She was dancing in the moonlight, hearing the waves swish softly against the shore, being whirled with the other dancers on the staircase out of the sea.

Waltzing.

Jake was actually doing proper ballroom dancing steps. Steps that she'd learned grudgingly as a teenager—and only because Charlie had been forced into having lessons and had begged her and Seb to go, too, to make it more bearable for him. She'd had to dance with greasy middle-aged men who'd leered at her, or boys her own age whose skin had been covered in spots. She'd hated every second of it and she'd only stuck it out for her brother's sake.

But this—this was different. The man holding her right now was only a couple of years older than she was. His cheek, pressed against hers, was freshly shaven, soft and perfectly smooth. His hair was clean and positively invited her to thread her fingers through it.

When he began to sing the words instead of just humming the tune, she was completely lost. Spellbound. She could have been dancing under the moonlight in that far-off land: she didn't even hear the scream of the seagulls or the music pumping out from the children's funfair.

All she was aware of was Jake.

And when he sang the last couple of words, holding her closer, she couldn't help turning her face slightly, so her cheek slid against his. He moved at the same time, and then their mouths were touching. Lightly. Tentatively. One small kiss. And another. And another. And then her mouth was opening beneath his, letting him deepen the kiss. Intense. Sweet. Hot. His mouth tasted slightly salty from the sea breeze that had whipped tiny droplets of salt water onto their skin. And she wanted to taste more of his skin, to find out how soft the skin was along his collar-bones, how responsive his body was to hers.

When the kiss ended, they both stood staring at each other. Jake looked as shocked as she felt. And as lost. Part of her wanted to fling herself into his arms and kiss the worries from his face—let him kiss the worries from her heart, too.

But Vicky Radley leaned on nobody. She was her own woman, and that was the way it was going to stay. 'We shouldn't have done that,' she said, hoping she sounded cool and professional—though she had a nasty feeling that she was hyperventilating.

He said nothing.

Wasn't he going to help her out here? 'I—I'm not looking for a relationship.'

His smile was grim. 'You're an Hon. and I'm a pleb. Don't worry, I already know I'm way out of your league.'

She shook her head. 'That's not what I meant. Class isn't important.'

'Isn't it?'

Oh, for goodness' sake! She could understand why Charlie hated being a baron when people reacted to you like this. 'It's who you are that counts, the way you behave towards others. It doesn't matter where you come from.'

'Then why?'

Why no relationships? She swallowed hard. 'I told you. I want to be a head of department. I want to be a professor. And I can't do that if I…if I'm not focused. If I let someone distract me.'

'I wouldn't distract you.'

Yes, he would. He'd already distracted her far too much. 'I don't have room in my life for a relationship.'

His gaze was still fixed on her mouth, as if he could still taste the kiss they'd just shared. 'Neither do I. I spend most of my free time raising funds for the unit.'

And she spent hers studying. Neither of them had space in their lives. So it wasn't going to happen.

Good.

'So that's settled, then,' she said.

He shook his head. 'I don't think this is going to go away, Vicky. I've been dreaming about you since the day I met you. Dreams that…' A flush stained his cheekbones. 'You don't need to know the details. Just that I can't stop thinking about you. I thought maybe we could be friends, that it would be enough for me. But it's not. And kissing you didn't break the spell, either.' A muscle tightened in his jaw. 'And don't say it's not the same for you. You look as if someone's just dropped you into a pool of ice-cold water.'

Which was exactly how she felt. She dragged in a breath. 'I can't do this, Jake. I know what I want to do in my life, and…'

'Why? Why can't we have it all?' Jake asked softly.

'You'd distract me,' she said again.

'Actually, you might find it an advantage.'

Her eyes widened. 'You mean, sleep with you and I'll get a promotion? That's disgusting!'

He took a step backwards, as if she'd slapped him, and his face darkened. 'That's not what I meant at all. But I've been a doctor for four years longer than you have. Worked in different hospitals. So I've dealt with cases you might not have come across, and maybe I could think up some really tough questions for you when you're studying.'

Advantages…as in being with someone who understood what she wanted to do. Someone who'd support her studying and help her expand her knowledge. Someone to bounce ideas off and discuss things with.

He'd already told her of his plans to develop the staff, through shadowing and mentoring as well as courses. She knew from working with him that he was friendly to everyone but hadn't tried it on with any of the staff. He wasn't a flirt or a tease. If he said something, he meant it. So why on earth had she said something so stupid?

Because she'd panicked.

Because she was scared that Jake would matter too much to her, if she allowed him near enough.

She counted to three. Slowly. To make sure her voice didn't wobble when she finally spoke. 'I owe you an apology. I jumped to conclusions.'

'The wrong ones,' he said, turning away from her. 'I'll drive you home.'

She realised she'd dropped the bear when he'd kissed her. She picked it up and dusted the sand off its fur, then followed Jake miserably back to the car. How had it all gone so wrong?

And that was exactly why she'd given up on relationships. Hers always ended up in a mess. Her boyfriends wanted to come first, not seeing that she needed to prove something to herself first— prove that she could make it right to the top. And when she hadn't been prepared to drop her studies for them, they'd walked away.

Just like Jake was walking away from her now.

By the time they reached the car, she'd made up her mind. 'You don't need to drop me home. I'll get the train back.'

He matched her for coolness. 'I have to drive myself back to London, so you may as well come with me.'

'I—'

'Just get in, Vicky.' He sounded tired. Hurt. Lost.

That made two of them.

She climbed into the car in silence. He didn't bother trying to engage her in conversation—he just turned up the volume on the stereo. Keith Urban was singing a song of love and loss, about being strong and letting go. Crying. Something Vicky never did. She always kept her self-control. Always.

So the dampness on her cheeks took her by surprise. And although she tried to rub it away without him noticing, he must have seen the movement of her hand out of the corner of his eye because he swore softly, turned into the next road and parked in the first available spot.

'What are you doing?' she asked.

'I've made you cry. And that's not how today was supposed to be. It was supposed to be fun. A way of saying thank you for your support.' He grimaced. 'And I did a Georgy Porgy on you.'

'Georgy Porgy?'

'Kissed the girl and made her cry.'

'I'm not crying because you kissed me.' She took a deep breath. 'I'm rubbish at this sort of thing. That's the other reason I don't date. I'm not good with people.'

He scoffed. 'No way. I've seen you with patients.'

'That's different—that's work. I'm talking about *outside* work.'

'Is that why you never go on team nights out?' he asked softly.

She nodded. 'I know what I'm like. I'll say the wrong thing and hurt someone's feelings. Like I hurt yours, just now. I… The only people I go out with are Seb and Charlie, because they know me well enough not to take offence. Except they're married now.'

'And their wives don't like you?'

She shook her head. 'Sophie and Alyssa are lovely. They accept me for who I am. But they want to give me a happy ending like theirs. And I can't face another Saturday night dinner party where I get paired off with someone they think would be right for me.'

'Someone you'd never pick for yourself in a million years.' Gently, he wiped away her tears with the pad of his thumb.

'And it's *not* because they're not posh enough for me—I'm not like that. It's because they don't understand. They want to come first.'

'And you're dedicated to your job.'

He didn't sound judgemental. He sounded as if he understood. 'It's the same for you?'

'Near enough. Except for me it's not studying, it's raising money for the unit. You can't run a marathon if you skip your training sessions.'

You couldn't get to the top of your particular specialty if you skipped your training sessions, either. So he knew exactly where she was coming from. Let your partner talk you into missing 'just one' session and it would snowball, and before you knew it you'd be a million miles away from where you'd planned to be. Vicky swallowed. 'I didn't mean what I said. About—about sleeping with you to get promoted.'

'And I shouldn't have snapped at you.'

'Apology accepted.'

'That wasn't an apology.' He leaned forward and kissed her lightly on the mouth, his lips just brushing hers. *'That* was an apology.'

She touched her mouth. It was tingling. Throbbing. As if she'd eaten a highly spiced meal and the spices had sensitised her skin. How could just the barest skim of his lips against hers do that?

Then she realised that he was waiting. 'Sorry. Did you say something?'

'No.'

'What, then?'

'I was just thinking…maybe you'd like to apologise, too.'

With a kiss.

He wanted her to kiss him.

'If that's what you want to do,' he added softly.

And he was giving her the choice.

Back off, and keep things as they were. Or lean forward and kiss him. Open herself up to the possibilities.

She wasn't scared of operating. Of the delicate job she did in Theatre, where the tiniest wrong move could have the most ghastly consequences. She had confidence there in spades. So why was she scared now?

To kiss, or not to kiss.

He was trying to keep his expression neutral, she could see that. But his eyes gave him away. Deep, dark and pleading.

She leaned forward. Touched her mouth lightly to his. Closed her eyes and waited for him to grab her—and, when nothing happened, opened her eyes and looked at him. His face was still very close to hers, and he was smiling.

'Not so bad, was it?' he whispered.

'No. It was all right.' More than all right. And her mouth was still tingling. Anticipation, perhaps. Of a longer kiss. Deeper. Hotter. Like the one they'd shared on the beach, only this time there wouldn't be anyone else around or any clothes as a barrier between them. Just the two of them between freshly laundered cotton sheets.

'Jake…' Her voice cracked.

He was insane. Utterly insane. That was the only possible reason why he took her hand and brought it to his lips. Kissed each finger in turn—still keeping his gaze steady on hers. 'I didn't intend this to happen. I really thought we could just be friends.' He brushed his lips against her fingers again. He loved just the touch of her skin against his mouth. Her clean scent. 'I don't do relationships. Especially with colleagues. I know how messy it can get.'

'So why now? Why me?'

Good question. Though he didn't have an answer. 'I've never met anyone who's had this sort of effect on me before.' And that in itself was scary. It meant he could be hurt. In all his previous relationships he'd managed to keep enough distance to be safe. But he had a nasty feeling that Vicky was going to matter to him. A lot. And it was already too late to back out. 'I want to see you, Vicky. But I'll respect your studies—just as

I know you'll respect my fundraising.' She'd already proved that to him. 'I'm not going to stand in the way of your career.'

'See me?' she asked softly.

He nodded. 'A relationship. The real thing. You and me. Dinner. Going to places together. Sharing things.' Making love. Not that he was going to say *that* right now. He didn't want to scare her off.

'What about work?'

He shrugged. 'So we work together. But we'll keep it quiet, if you'd prefer. It's nothing to do with anyone else anyways. Just you and me.'

'Just you and me,' she echoed.

He waited. If he pushed too hard now, she'd run. She was clearly as thrown by this as he was. But the way she'd kissed him on the beach…he was sure she felt the same pull. And the same fear of letting go enough to act on that attraction. Was she brave enough to give it a try?

Her fingers tightened round his, and her eyes were very, very blue. 'This feels like jumping out of a plane without a parachute.'

'That's how we know we're alive,' he whispered.

'If you help me with my studying, I have to help you with your training?'

And take time out of her schedule? He shook his head. 'Not unless you want to. But if we're on the same shift, maybe we could swim together before work. And there's always multi-tasking.'

'Multi-tasking?'

'Running and studying at the same time. If you're training properly, you should be able to hold a conversation. So I can test you on your knowledge as we run.'

She smiled. 'You have all the answers.'

He shook his head. 'I'm improvising. I don't know where this is going any more than you do. And it scares me just as much as it scares you. Only...I think not seeing you is marginally more scary.'

She said nothing.

Quietly, he released her hand. 'No pressure, Vicky. I'll give you time to think about it. If you choose not to see me, I'll accept that and I won't make a fuss. And if you choose to say yes—' please, please, let her say yes '—I'll cook you dinner at my place.' He paused. 'What shift are you on tomorrow?'

'Late.'

'Day after?'

'Early.'

He nodded. 'Day after tomorrow. Half past seven.' A little over forty-eight hours. That was giving her time, wasn't it?

And somehow, he had to get through the next two days.

## CHAPTER SEVEN

THEY were on different shifts the next day, and Jake didn't get a chance to talk to Vicky. She didn't leave him a message either, so he had no idea what her decision was—or if she'd even made a decision. On Friday morning, she wasn't at the gym before her shift.

Was she avoiding him? Or was he just being paranoid?

When he did see Vicky, on the ward, she was her normal self. Cool, calm and professional. Jake had to fight hard to behave the same way; inwardly, he was a mess. Scared in case she said no. Excited in case she said yes. And so very, very aware of her physical presence. Even with the whole length of the ward between them, he could feel the touch of her skin. A memory so real it was tangible.

But memories weren't enough. He wanted more. So much more.

*Please, let her say yes.*

He managed to snap his control back into place during clinic, particularly when his first case was a baby.

Jeanette Saunders was sitting with her tiny baby in her arms, looking anxious. 'My husband said I was fussing over nothing, but my health visitor said I ought to get the baby checked out.'

An urgent referral: Jake had already read the notes. 'One of her eyelids is drooping?'

Jeanette bit her lip. 'That normally means a stroke, doesn't it? Our next-door neighbour had a stroke last year. But Tabitha's too young to have had a stroke!'

She was clearly on the verge of tears. Jake smiled reassuringly at her. 'A droopy eyelid could be all sorts of things. It could be a problem with a muscle or a nerve. Can I have a look at her?'

Jeanette nodded.

'Tabitha's a very pretty name.'

'It means "gazelle". We found it in the baby name book.'

Jake kept her chatting while he looked at the baby. Tabitha's left upper eyelid was indeed droopy—and there were a couple of associated signs that told him exactly what the problem was.

'Tabitha has something called Horner's syndrome,' he explained. 'It's a condition where the upper eyelid droops—you might hear medics talking about ptosis, which is the medical name for it. Look at her left eye—the pupil is smaller and her iris is slightly lighter. That tells me it's a congenital condition.'

'You mean, it's hereditary? Tabby got it from us?'

Jake shook his head. 'No, it means it happened around the time of the birth or even in the womb.'

'What causes it?'

'We don't always know. Sometimes it's caused by trauma, sometimes by a medical condition such as migraine, or sometimes just in the way the blood vessels develop as the baby grows. Basically, there's a blockage which interrupts the sympathetic nerve supply to the eye, somewhere between the beginning of the nerve in the brain and the end of the nerve in the eye.'

Jeanette's face crumpled. 'We had a difficult

birth. I wanted to do it myself, but I couldn't—I had to have forceps in the end.'

'Don't blame yourself,' Jake said immediately. 'It might have nothing to do with the forceps.'

'Can it—can it be cured?' Jeanette asked.

He knew what she was really asking. *Is my baby going to die?*

'If there's an underlying medical condition that can be treated, then, yes, it can be cured. If it's congenital, then, no—but it doesn't mean she can't live a completely normal life. I'll need to do some tests first so I can be sure of the cause. It's going to mean a bit of hanging around, I'm afraid, while the eye drops work.'

'I don't mind. Just as long as she's all right.' The last word was almost a sob.

'It's always worrying when your little one has to come to hospital,' Jake said gently. 'Is she your first?'

Jeanette nodded.

'She's beautiful. And we'll do our best for her, I promise you. Now, what I'm going to do is put some eye drops in to see how Tabitha's pupils dilate. It's not going to hurt but it might sting a tiny bit and she might want a bit of a cuddle. Can you hold her for me while I put the drops in, please?' He could have asked a nurse to do it, but he thought that giving Jeanette something practical to do might help take her mind off her worries.

He put four per cent cocaine drops in both eyes: the right pupil dilated, but the left didn't. 'It's Horner's syndrome,' he said, 'but I need to find out where the blockage is.' He decided not to mention the possibility of a brain scan at that point—he'd only need to do that if the interruption to the nerve was preganglionic, somewhere in the brain stem or spinal cord, and there was no point in worrying Jeanette unnecessarily.

The next set of drops were one per cent hydrox-amphetamine: again, the right pupil dilated, and the left didn't. He breathed a sigh of relief. 'What that test tells me is that the interruption to the nerve supply is what we call postganglionic—that means it's somewhere between the root of Tabitha's neck and her eye, not in her brain stem or spinal cord. I want to do one more test, though, to be absolutely sure.'

The final set of drops were 1:1000 adrenaline

drops. Only the left pupil dilated this time. 'It's absolutely definitely postganglionic,' he said, 'and it's something that happened around the birth, not something that's happened over time.'

'So it can't be cured? Tabby will always have a drooping eye?'

'It shouldn't bother her or affect her development—and the health visitor did the right thing in sending her here to check it wasn't caused by a serious medical condition,' Jake said. 'If you find the way the eye looks upsets her when she's older, we can operate—I can arrange for her to see a plastic surgeon.' He stroked the baby's cheek with the backs of his fingers. 'But she'll be fine. Won't you, beautiful?' The baby's eyes were a gorgeous colour. Slate- blue.

Like Vicky's.

His stomach clenched. *Please, let her say yes.*

He made it through to the end of clinic. He'd overrun slightly, so he only had enough time to grab a sandwich before his afternoon clinic began. Vicky, predictably, was nowhere in sight—either on a ward round or in clinic herself, he presumed.

No message from her on his desk.

Swallowing his disappointment, he flicked into his email inbox. Just in case.

Nothing.

OK. So she was going to say no. He was an adult. He could handle it.

He forced himself to focus on his afternoon clinic. Headed back to his desk to write up notes and referral letters. At six o'clock—well after his shift should have ended—he flicked into his email.

And there it was.

A message from Vicky.

The official 'thanks, but no thanks' note. OK. He would read it, delete it and move on.

He opened the message, skimmed it and had already pressed 'delete' when he realised what it said.

With a yelp, he switched to the 'deleted' folder and retrieved the message.

*7.30's fine. Can you text me your address, please?* And she'd left him her mobile phone number.

He punched the air. She was going to give them a chance!

And then his smile faded. It was six o'clock on a Friday night. He hadn't gone shopping for food yet, in case he jinxed things. His flat was a mess. And Vicky was coming to dinner in an hour and a half.

He scribbled her number onto a piece of paper, double-checked that he'd written it down correctly, logged off everything in his office, tucked his paperwork into his briefcase and headed for the outside of the hospital at a run. As soon as he was outside, he switched on his mobile phone, punched in her number and waited for her to answer.

'The mobile phone you are calling is currently unavailable.'

Oh, no. Oh, no, no, no. The worst thing he could have heard.

He'd been so convinced she'd say no he hadn't even thought what to cook. She'd refused a bacon sandwich…was she vegetarian? No, she'd eaten fish and chips. Maybe she just didn't eat meat.

And because her phone was either switched off or she was in an area with a poor signal, he couldn't talk to her to check her food likes and dislikes.

OK. He knew she ate fish. He'd play it safe. He sent a text giving her his address, then rushed to the supermarket nearest to his flat.

The stuffed mushrooms took hardly any time to prepare. The fish could marinate while he frantically cleared up. Pudding was simple and only needed to be prepared about thirty seconds before they ate it. Plus, he'd cheated and bought a bottle of wine from the chiller cabinet, so it would at least be at the right temperature.

He just hoped she wasn't the sort who'd be early. Please, let her be five minutes late. Late enough for him to have his flat looking reasonable and himself looking presentable, but not late enough to make him panic that she wasn't going to turn up at all.

Just as well he used an electric razor instead of insisting on a wet shave. He shaved with his left hand while his right hand tidied things away. When he'd finished, he had barely enough time for a very, very quick shower and to change into casual black trousers and a round-necked, light-weight cream sweater.

He'd just put the mushrooms in the oven when the doorbell rang.

Seven-thirty precisely.

Oh, Lord. He felt like a teenager on his first

date. Not a thirty-five-year-old consultant who'd had a few relationships, though nothing serious. Maybe he'd been hexed and something had switched his body with that of a fifteen-year-old, full of pimples and raging hormones—like one of the 'body swap' movies that had been so popular during his late teens.

Shut up, Jake, he told himself fiercely, and opened the door.

'Hi.'

He was lost for words. Vicky was wearing a little black dress and pearls, and her hair was loose. He'd never seen her hair loose—at the pool, she always wore a cap, and even at the seaside she'd worn it in the same style she wore it for work, caught back at the nape of her neck and pulled tight enough to be severe.

Loose, it was even more beautiful than he'd imagined. Dark waves. Glossy, silky, bouncy hair. Hair he wanted to play with. It was all he could do not to haul her over his shoulder, carry her to his bed and spread her hair all over his pillow before undressing her very, very slowly and kissing her all over.

'You look lovely,' he said, and could have kicked himself when he heard his voice squeaking. He sounded like a kid whose voice was breaking. Damn. He was meant to sound sophisticated and urbane. The kind of man a woman like Vicky would be attracted to.

'Thank you.' She handed him a box. 'I, um, wasn't sure what you were cooking, so I didn't bring wine. And flowers don't seem the right thing to bring a man.'

Flowers? Oh-h. He could think of something to do with flowers. Preferably roses. And preferably involving her naked body.

Uh. He really hoped he hadn't said that out loud.

'Thank you,' he said politely. Then he looked at the box. 'Oh, *yes*.' Hand-made chocolates. He grinned. 'You'll have to bully me into sharing these. And even then it might not work.'

She grinned back. 'You're as bad as Seb.'

Jealousy had started to flicker at the back of his neck when she added, 'My middle brother.'

He remembered his manners. 'Come in. Can I get you a drink?'

She shook her head. 'Thanks, but I'm driving.'

'Sorry. I should have told you to get a taxi.' He frowned. 'Hang on, you were on an early today. You're not on call?'

'Um, no.'

At least her pager wasn't going to bleep in the middle of their meal. That was one good thing.

'Mineral water?' he asked. At her nod, he added, 'Still or sparkling?'

'Sparkling, please.'

He ushered her into the kitchen, then lit the candle in the centre of his dining table. Vanilla—though the scent would be overpowered by the aroma of herbs and balsamic vinegar from the oven.

'Something smells nice,' Vicky said.

'I hope you like it. I did try to ring you to check if there was anything you really hated, apart from bacon.'

He sounded as panicky as she felt. And no wonder. She'd left it so long before saying yes that he'd had to do everything at the last minute. Bad-mannered didn't even begin to cover her behaviour. 'Sorry. I should have let you know earlier. Except…' Could she admit that she'd been too scared to make up her mind until the very end of her shift, and then she'd emailed him in a rush before she'd lost her nerve?

'I was in clinic all day,' Jake said, rescuing her. 'I thought you were going to say no.'

'So did I,' she said. And she'd nearly chickened out on the drive here.

'What made you change your mind?' he asked softly.

She had no answer to that. And he didn't push her. He just said, 'I'm glad you did.'

Me, too, she thought.

'Dinner's going to be about another ten minutes.' He slid a loaf of bread into the oven. 'Want the guided tour?'

'Sure.'

'Kitchen-diner,' he said, indicating the room they were standing in. He ushered her into the hall. 'Bathroom.' Small, but very tidy and colour-washed in a relaxing shade of aqua. 'My room.' He indicated a door but didn't open it. No pressure, then. 'Living room.'

The room was small, but the thing that really struck her was how many CDs there were in the floor-to-ceiling tower units standing against one wall. He didn't have a TV: he had a piano. A very, very good sound system. A few shelves of books, mainly medical texts. And what looked like an extremely comfortable sofa.

'You play?' she asked, knowing it was a stupid question even before she asked it. She already knew he was musical—the way he'd sung to her at the beach had told her that. Plus, his mother had been a musician: the chances were he'd inherited his mother's musical ability.

'Not good enough to be professional, but well enough to keep me amused.' He paused. 'The piano was my mum's. That, her wedding ring and a few photos are all I've got of her and Dad. And memories. She used to play to me when I was little, sing me songs.'

Seeing the flash of pain on his face, she placed her hand on his arm. It was meant to be a comforting touch…except it left her feeling as if an electric current had thrummed through her.

A feeling he shared, judging by the look in his eyes.

She had to keep her hands off. Now.

'Did your mum make any records?'

'One or two. But she wasn't well known outside the club circuit. That tour in America was meant to be her big break.'

Except it had broken her life, instead. 'That's a shame.'

'It happens. I had her for twelve years.' He shrugged. 'That's more than some people get.'

And he was clearly trying so hard not to be bitter about it. 'Um, it's a nice flat,' she said, hoping to find a less painful topic of conversation for him.

He shrugged. 'Tiny, but it does me.' He showed her back to the kitchen.

The first course was gorgeous. Mushrooms stuffed with a mixture of breadcrumbs, garlic and butter, with warm ciabatta bread on the side to dip into the juices. The second course was impressive: salmon, baked with what she suspected was lime zest and butter, with tiny new potatoes and a mixture of baked Mediterranean vegetables.

But pudding... Pudding was to die for. Fresh raspberries, with creamy yoghurt poured over and a sprinkling of brown sugar on the top, flashed under the grill until it caramelised.

'That was fabulous. Even if it's hell on the arteries.'

'Wrong. It's nought per cent fat Greek yoghurt.' He grinned. 'Well, I have to keep the rest of my diet healthy, to make up for my sweet tooth.'

'Chocolate.' She eyed the box and remembered what he'd said. 'Which you're going to share with me.'

Jake spooned coffee into the cafetière and took a carton of milk from the fridge. 'You can have *one*. If you're a good girl.'

She didn't feel like being a good girl right now. She propped her elbows on the table, linked her fingers together and rested her chin on her hands. 'What if I'm a bad girl?' she asked huskily.

# CHAPTER EIGHT

Jake promptly dropped the milk, and it went everywhere. He groaned and grabbed a cloth to mop up. 'Couldn't you have waited until my hands were empty before you said something like that?'

'Sorry.'

Vicky didn't sound it. She was laughing. Though he thought she was laughing with him rather than at him.

He finished mopping up, then turned to face her, leaning back against the worktop. 'So. You're a *bad* girl.'

She moistened her lower lip, and his pulse speeded up another notch.

'I could be.' Her voice was low, soft and seductive.

Considering neither of them had touched a drop of wine—she'd refused even half a glass, so he'd joined her in drinking sparkling mineral water—it wasn't alcohol blurring his senses like this.

It was Vicky. Just Vicky.

'How bad?' He had to know.

'How bad do you want me to be?'

Very, *very* bad. 'Come here, and I'll tell you.'

For a moment he thought she was going to stay where she was. But then she stood up, kicked off her shoes and walked towards him. He opened his arms, and she was there. Right where he wanted her to be. Up close and personal, her body pressed against his, her glorious hair sliding through his fingers and her arms round his waist.

'This bad,' he whispered, nuzzling the curve of her neck. He didn't recognise her perfume, and he assumed it was something exclusive—something suitable for the daughter of a baron. Whatever it was, he loved it. 'This bad.' He brushed his mouth against hers.

Such a light kiss. So gentle, so sweet. But it blew his self-control to smithereens. 'This bad,' he said, and unzipped the back of her dress.

Lord, her skin was soft. He wanted to touch.

Look. Taste. He stroked his way down her spine, and nuzzled the strap of her dress off one shoulder.

'Jake.'

Her voice was no more than a whisper, but he stopped. Instantly. 'I'm sorry. I...I don't normally do this sort of thing.' He hardly knew her. And here he was, undressing her. In his *kitchen*. How tacky could he get?

She stroked his face. 'That isn't what I meant.'

He met her gaze, and was rewarded with a glint of mischief. *What if I'm a bad girl?* The tight knot of shame and misery eased. 'So what did you mean?'

'If you're planning to take off my dress—'

All the blood in his body went south at the thought.

'—then I think I should get to undress you, too.'

He lost the ability to speak. He didn't dare say a word, knowing it would just come out as a caveman grunt.

Caveman.

That was it. The only thing he could do. He picked her up—disregarding the fact that she was nearly as tall as he was—and carried her to his bedroom.

'You troglodyte,' Vicky teased, and licked his earlobe.

Oh, yes. He was definitely a caveman where she was concerned. He set her back down on her feet, but made sure every part of her body slid against every part of his. Just so she knew exactly what she was letting herself in for.

'Your dress.' He couldn't get the rest of the words out. But his face must have said it all for him, because she gave him a slow, bad-girl smile. Took one step backwards. Pushed the other shoulder strap down and let her dress fall to the floor.

Jake quivered. Her underwear was black and lacy. And she was wearing hold-up stockings. She looked utterly delectable and he wanted her right now.

'Uh-uh.' She held up a warning finger before he could step towards her. 'Your turn.'

'You said you wanted to undress me yourself.'

'So I did.' She swivelled her hand and the warning finger beckoned him instead.

He knew he had a silly grin on his face. He didn't care. Because they were about to do something he'd been dreaming about for over a month. He stepped forward. Stopped right in front of her.

She tugged at the hem of his sweater, and he lifted his arms to make it easy for her.

'Mmm.' She ran her fingers over his pecs. 'So you swim every day?'

'Most days. It relaxes me.'

She made an appreciative murmur and traced his ribcage. 'Very, very nice.'

He swallowed. 'Do I get to…?' To do the same to her?

She smiled. 'Do you want to?'

'Oh, yeah.' His voice was so deep, it was almost a purr.

He had to be dreaming this. He was in his flat, yes, but he was still waiting for Vicky to turn up. Any minute now, the door buzzer would break into this fantasy and he'd realise that she wasn't undoing the button of his trousers and he wasn't sliding the straps of her bra down her arms. Any second now, he'd hear her cool, calm, professional tones saying something very polite. Something a million miles away from the husky, breathy voice in his ear saying, 'Touch me, Jake.'

Any millisecond now.

Her bra dropped to the floor and his fingers touched soft, smooth skin. Alabaster, all over—except warm and giving, not cold and hard. So Vicky

Radley wasn't a sunbather. Fine by him. He'd rather be the one to kiss her skin, not the sun.

She had perfect nipples, dusky rose, which hardened as she waited for his mouth to trail down from the pulse hammering in her neck. A long, slow journey to paradise for both of them.

Which started right now.

She gave a soft murmur of surprise and pleasure as he tipped her onto his bed, dropping to his knees beside her at the same time. 'So beautiful,' he breathed. 'So beautiful, it hurts.'

'Yes, you are,' she whispered.

She thought *he* was beautiful?

Yep. He was definitely dreaming this. But what a dream. And he was going to enjoy every last moment of it. Slowly, he trailed his tongue down the valley between her breasts. Kissed the soft undersides. And finally took one hard nipple into his mouth and sucked.

She was beautiful. Perfect. All his. Vicky Radley was here lying on his bed, wearing next to nothing, and her fingers were threaded through his hair, urging him on as he kissed his way down her body. She was making tiny little noises of pleasure, and he could tell just how shallow and fast her breathing was.

Like his own. Almost hyperventilating, he wanted her so much.

He nuzzled lower. Stroked her thighs. Slid one finger under the hem of her knickers. She was warm, wet and so very ready for him. Just as he was ready for her.

'Is this really happening?' he couldn't help asking.

'I think so.' She sounded so much cooler and calmer than he felt. And then she added, 'I hope so.' There was a slight break in her voice. So, Jake thought, that meant she felt the same way. Thrown off balance. Wanting. Needing. Crazy.

But Vicky wasn't a bad girl. She was a nice girl. Which meant he shouldn't be doing this. At least, not without giving her a chance to say no, without any pressure. And what had he done? He'd carried her into his bedroom. He hadn't given her a choice.

This was going to be tough—especially if she said no—but it was too important to rush. He wasn't going to sacrifice a long-term goal for a short-term aim. He shifted to sit beside her on the bed. 'Vicky. You don't have to do this.'

'Yes, I do.'

'Why?' He frowned. 'You don't have to prove anything.'

'I know. But if you and I don't…' She shivered. 'I think I'm going to spontaneously combust.'

'You're sure about this?'

In answer, she took his hand, kissed each knuckle, then placed it on her naked breast.

Suddenly, there wasn't any air left in the room. The only way he could breathe was to kiss her. Now. And she was kissing him back. Touching him. Exploring him. Driving him well over the edge of reason.

The next thing he knew, he was kneeling between her thighs, seeing her hair spread over his pillow exactly the way he'd wanted it to be. Dark, silky waves over the pure white cotton.

And then his common sense kicked in. Yes, he wanted her. Very badly. He could hardly wait—but they had to be sensible about this. Use a condom.

He just hoped he still had some. And that they were within date.

'Um, forgive me a moment…' He rummaged in his drawer. Where the hell was a box of condoms when you needed it?

He hadn't made any assumptions about tonight. He'd said dinner and he'd meant dinner. Yes, he'd hoped she kiss him. Hold him close. But he hadn't thought they'd end up here, in his bed. Naked. Making love.

'Problem?' she asked.

He may as well come clean. 'I wasn't planning to seduce you. I might not, um, be prepared.' But this was the twenty-first century. Women carried condoms nowadays, didn't they? 'Unless you have something?'

She shook her head. 'I hadn't planned this either. It was meant to be dinner. Time to get to know each other a bit better.'

'Maybe a little kissing,' he suggested.

She smiled. 'And maybe you dancing with me again.'

She'd liked that, then? So had he. Dancing cheek to cheek on sun-warmed sand. And it didn't matter if it was Southend-on-Sea on a rainy English spring day or some exotic tropical island. Just as long as they were together.

*Why was it taking so long to find the damned condom?* Maybe he should learn to be tidy instead of cramming everything into a drawer and jamming it closed.

At last. The little foil packet was right at the back. Right at the bottom. And if it was out of date, he was going to implode with frustration. The whole of London would hear him scream.

His hands were shaking as he turned it over and found the all-important figures. 'Yes,' he breathed in relief.

'I hope that's a "yes" to what I think it is.'

He smiled wryly. 'Yes, I've found it. And, yes, it's within date. We're safe.'

'So you don't—?' She stopped, and shook her head, as if embarrassed that she'd started to ask.

Actually, he was flattered that she cared enough to want to know. 'I date. Sometimes I sleep with my dates, if there's mutual attraction. But there's been nobody permanent. Nobody long term. And there hasn't been anyone for a while. So, no, I don't usually carry a huge stock of condoms just on the off-chance some nurse will want to drape herself all over me.' He waited a beat. Yeah, he understood that flicker of jealousy. Only too well. It was knifing into him right now. 'You?'

'I date when my brothers bully me into it.'

And the rest of it? Was this 'bad girl Vicky'—the one lying naked in his bed with her hair spread over his pillow and giving him a come-hither look—someone that other people got to see?

It must have been written over his face, because she smiled bleakly. 'I haven't dated for a while. Can't remember the last time I slept with someone. And maybe this is a bad idea. Maybe I should go home.'

He sucked in a breath. 'No pressure, Vicky. If you want to go home, I won't stop you.' He'd spend the night almost howling in frustration, but he wasn't the sort of man who'd expect a sexual payment for dinner.

Though he wasn't going to let her go thinking he'd changed his mind about her. 'If you say no, I'll understand. But if it's a yes and you want to stay, I might have to do a cartwheel and whoop a bit.'

'A cartwheel?' Her mouth twitched. 'Right here?'

OK. So his flat was small and the bed took up most of the space in the room—nobody older than three years old could have done a cartwheel there. 'An imaginary cartwheel,' he amended.

'I have a better idea,' she said. 'A much, much better idea.'

His heart stopped at the look in her eyes. That sexy pout. That 'come here, baby' smile. 'What?'

'Let's go back to plan A. Where we were.'

'You're sure about this?'

'No,' she admitted, 'but I let my head rule me ninety-nine point nine per cent of the time. Maybe it's time I tried something different.'

'I promise you,' Jake said softly, 'you're not going to regret this.' Who cared if he was out of practice? He'd improvise. Explore. Find out just where and how she liked being touched. Licked. Nibbled.

He leaned over to kiss her. Instant fire. Wherever he touched her, his hands tingled. Wherever she touched him, his skin tingled. It was as if every nerve was flaring with light. And by the time he sheathed himself in a condom and slipped inside her, Jake's whole body felt ablaze with light and energy. Every kiss, every touch just turned up the voltage. White heat. As he lost himself in her, he looked into her eyes—and the same blazing wonder was reflected right back at him.

Paradise.

\* \* \*

Vicky lay on her side, curled into Jake's body, her head pillowed on his shoulder. She had no idea what time it was, and she didn't care. Tonight her books could wait. Tomorrow could take care of itself. Right now, she was where she wanted to be. In Jake's bed. Wrapped in his arms. Skin to skin. Breathing in the clean, pure scent of his body.

He'd been a considerate lover. He'd made sure he'd found exactly where and how she liked to be touched. Kissed. Tasted. And although she wasn't a virgin, she might as well have been—tonight was like nothing else she'd ever experienced.

'OK?' he asked softly.

'Very OK.' She snuggled closer, not wanting to talk. Not wanting to break the spell. Not wanting to go back to real life.

'Good.' He stroked her hair. 'Stay with me tonight?'

Spend the night with him.

More love-making.

Oh, it was tempting. She wanted more, more, more of that rush of pleasure. As if someone had shrunk her to a centimetre high, balanced her on the cork of a champagne bottle, shaken the bottle and then just let the cork fly.

But, as she'd told him earlier, her head ruled for ninety-nine point nine per cent of the time. And spending the night with Jake Lewis would be the first step on a very slippery slope. A slope that would lead directly away from the peak of the career she wanted.

A step she wasn't ready to take. Might never be ready to take.

As if he'd guessed what she was thinking, he said softly, 'It's not part of a master plan to get you married, pregnant and working part time at the very most in a very junior role.'

Was she that obvious? 'Of course not.'

'Though I should warn you, that was my last condom.'

He must have felt the tension in her body, because he kissed the top of her head. 'Relax. Yes, I want to make love with you again. A lot. Now I've found out what it's like being with you, going back to a colleagues-only relationship isn't an option for me. I want you. Very, very badly. But I'm never going to stand in your way, Vicky. I know your career comes first. And that's fine, as long as you have room for me in your life as well.'

'A relationship.'

She hadn't realised she'd spoken aloud until he laughed. 'Vicky, I don't sleep with anyone on a first date—and this is officially our first date, because that day at the seaside doesn't count.'

'I don't sleep with anyone on a first date, either.'

'I know.' He smoothed his hand along the curve of her waist and hip. 'Though you make an excellent bad girl.'

She'd started all this. He'd offered her dinner. Meaning just dinner. *She'd* been the one to suggest something more. And he'd given her several opportunities to back out. Even when he'd been aroused and ready to rip the condom packet open, he'd given her the choice to go.

She hadn't.

Which made her…cheap. She'd thrown herself at him.

Again, he seemed to read her mood without any effort. 'I respect my extremely competent colleague, Dr Radley. I'm a little intimidated by the Honourable Victoria Radley, though I've spent the past month fantasising about her, a box of straw-berries and a single red rose.'

She wasn't sure what he had in mind, but a surge of pure desire flowed through her body at his words. She had a feeling that Jake would be a very, very inventive lover.

'And as for Vicky the bad girl…she makes me weak at the knees. She's the sexiest woman I've ever, ever met. Even the way she smiles turns me into a puddle of desire.' His voice was husky now, sultry. 'And she can have her way with me any time she chooses. Any time, any place. I'm all hers.'

If he kissed her now, she'd stay the night. What-ever her head said. She'd stay and make love with him. Touch. Taste. Learn every inch of his body, every mole and every crease.

When she said nothing, he sighed. 'What I'm try-ing to say, Vicky, is that I like you, I respect you, and I'm delighted that you've shared a very secret part of you with me. I'm not going to kiss and tell. If you want to keep us quiet at work, that's fine by me—though I couldn't give a damn about the hos-pital grapevine. People might talk, but someone else will knock us off the hot spot within a couple of days.'

True.

'I want to see you, Vicky. I want to spend time with you. I want to sit in the back row of the movies with you and an enormous bucket of popcorn. I want to walk hand in hand in Kew Gardens with you. Kiss you in a secluded corner. Drive out to the country with you and watch the stars. Go to a fireworks display with you on Bonfire Night, and take you home and see them happen all over again when we make love.' He paused. 'And I want to throw a party for my woman when she becomes professor of neurology.'

He'd called her his woman. He wanted to make love with her and see stars. And he saw her as professor of neurology.

*He believed in her.*

Her eyes filled with tears. 'I can't stay tonight.'

He smiled and traced her lower lip with the pad of his thumb. 'You're probably right. We're both on duty tomorrow—and if you stay here neither of us will get any sleep. Even if we don't have any more condoms between us.'

Her eyes widened. He was prepared to take risks like that?

He grinned, clearly guessing what she'd thought. 'There are other ways. I *could* give you an example right now.' He shifted to kiss her lightly on the mouth. 'Though I won't push you until you're ready.'

Her body tingled at the thought.

'But I'm going to keep asking you to stay. Because, one morning, I want to wake up with you in my arms.'

She wanted that, too. But even if he believed in her now, would he change? Would he be like her previous boyfriends at heart, want her to be something else and give up her dreams of a professorship? Like everyone she'd ever known—except for Seb and Charlie—trying to put her in a pigeonhole where she didn't want to be?

This was where she knew she should tell him that tonight was a one-off. That they couldn't carry on. That from now on their relationship was colleagues-only. And then she found herself saying, 'I'll cook dinner at my place, tomorrow night.'

He smiled. 'Thank you. I accept.' He kissed the tip of her nose. 'And you'd better go. While I still have the strength of will not to kidnap you and keep you in my bed until dawn.'

She wasn't sure if that was a threat or promise. And the fact that she wanted it, too, scared her even more. This wasn't supposed to happen.

Tomorrow. She'd cook him dinner, and she'd tell him tomorrow.

She wriggled out of bed and dressed swiftly. Her dress was creased to the point of embarrassment, but it didn't matter: she was driving home, so nobody would see. The dry-cleaner would make her dress pristine again.

Even the thought of it had her back in brisk, efficient neurologist mode. And well-mannered guest. 'I should help you wash up before I go.'

'Give me a kiss goodnight, and I'll let you off,' Jake said.

Lord, he was tempting. Lying there in the bed they'd just rumpled between them, his dark hair messy and his dark eyes laughing and his mouth looking so kissable. And was that a hickey on his collar-bone? Had *she* done that?

Oh, Lord.

She couldn't remember ever losing her control like that before. The few times she'd had sex, it had been all right—but not like tonight. Not that wild, fizzing, sweet feeling through her veins. Just looking at him sent shivers of desire running through her, as her body remembered how the way he'd touched her, the way she'd touched him, drove her crazy.

But tonight she was going to be sensible. She'd lost her head, yes, but she'd found it again. And now she was going to go home and study.

'Goodnight,' she said quietly, and leaned over to kiss him.

It was meant to be one little kiss. A gentle brush of her mouth against his. But he caught her lower lip between his, nibbled it, and Vicky almost ripped off her clothes and crawled back between the sheets with him then and there. With an effort, she pulled herself away. 'I have to go home.' Even though half of her didn't want to.

'I know.'

'I'll…see you tomorrow.'

'At work.' He smiled. 'Don't worry. Everything's

going to be fine. This is just between you and me. Nothing's going to change between us on the ward.'

And that, Vicky thought wryly, was almost what she was afraid of.

# CHAPTER NINE

ANYONE who saw Jake smile at Vicky the next morning would assume he was merely greeting a colleague. He was completely professional. Nobody would ever believe that less than twelve hours ago she'd been in his bed, making incoherent noises of pleasure as he'd brought her to climax.

The memory made her blush. She just hoped that nobody had noticed it through her make-up. But nobody, even their sharp-eyed colleague Gemma, asked any awkward questions. So maybe, just maybe, this was going to work out all right.

Maybe she wouldn't have to give him up.

When she came off shift, there was a message on her mobile phone. *7.30?* She texted back *yes*, and headed for the supermarket. He'd cooked for her last night. Tonight, she was going to show him what she could do.

\* \* \*

Jake paid the taxi driver and stood by the steps to Vicky's flat. It was crazy, feeling this nervous. But he'd told her the truth last night. The Honourable Victoria Radley was just a little bit intimidating. Especially as she lived in a posh mansion flat in the most fashionable part of Chelsea.

Stupid. He'd picked her up from here the day he'd taken her to the seaside. He shouldn't feel so out of place. And maybe he'd feel better if he knew who she would be tonight. The Honourable Victoria? Professional, cool Dr Radley? Or would she be his warm and sensual Bad Girl Vicky?

There was only one way to find out.

He pressed the buzzer and waited.

'Jake?' She sounded slightly breathless. As nervous he was, maybe?

'Uh-huh.'

'Come up. I'm on the top floor.'

He pushed the front door open after he heard the buzz, and took the stairs up to the fifth floor. She was waiting for him at the top.

The Honourable Victoria. In another little black dress—she probably had dozens of designer dresses in her wardrobe—wearing a string of matched pearls, and with her hair piled on top of her head. Cool, beautiful and remote. The kind of woman you'd give diamonds and orchids.

What he'd brought her was entirely out of place.

It slammed straight into his gut. So much for his bravado on her doorstep. Now he was a real fish out of water, gasping for his natural element. He didn't belong here, any more than the Honourable Victoria belonged in his tiny flat.

And then he noticed Vicky's hands. Her fingers were linked together and her knuckles were white. She was as nervous as he was.

So everything was going to be all right. They'd get through this—together.

He smiled, walked up to her and kissed her cheek. 'Hello, beautiful.'

'Hi.'

'I wish I'd brought you orchids now.' He handed her the huge bunch of bright pink gerberas.

She smiled. 'I hate orchids. And I love these. Thank you. Come in. Can I get you a drink?'

'Thank you. Whatever you're having.' He followed her through into the flat. The carpet was the type you actually sank into, the pictures on the walls were original watercolours, and the furniture had the kind of patina that only came with age. Furniture that had probably been in her family for generations. Her high-ranking, posh family.

Way, way, way out of his league.

Even the wineglass she handed him was posh. Lead crystal, so thin and fine he was almost scared to take a sip in case the glass shattered. His confidence deserted him again and he watched in silence as she arranged the gerberas on her kitchen window-sill—in a deceptively simple vase that had probably cost a fortune.

'They're lovely. Thank you,' she said, smiling at him.

'Pleasure.' He hated the stiff formality, but he really didn't know what else to say.

'My turn to give you the guided tour?' she suggested.

When she showed him around, he felt even more awkward. His entire flat would probably fit into two of the rooms here! The kitchen had proper terracotta tiles, hand-made wooden cabinets, granite worktops, top-of-the-range electrical equipment.

A million miles away from his cheap and cheerful kitchen. And she had a proper dining room rather than a corner of the kitchen to eat in; the antique table was set with silver, lead crystal, white porcelain and damask napkins in silver rings. He'd just bet she set the table properly like this every night, even if it was only for herself.

Her bathroom was enormous, too. Though when he noticed that the bath was big enough for two people, he had a tough job convincing his libido to shut up: it was sitting up, begging and whining loudly.

Her spare bedrooms—doubles, he noticed—both had deep pile carpets: one had a *bateau lit* and the other a wrought-iron bedstead. Both had pure white bedding—real high-maintenance stuff. And both smelled of lavender. Either she had a housekeeper who did it for her, or she was just very, very organised. Both were very probable: he wouldn't hazard a guess. And Lord only knew what her bedroom was like because she—following his lead, last night—didn't show him behind the closed door.

This was a mansion flat—and inside it *felt* like a mansion, too.

Though what else should he have expected from the Honourable Victoria Radley?

Her living room was a surprise and yet exactly what he'd expected. Bookshelves stuffed with medical texts and classic fiction—all arranged strictly in alphabetical order, he noticed—a desk with a halogen lamp and what looked like a state-of-the-art laptop, an overstuffed sofa. But there were other surprises: a shelf full of DVDs, mainly musicals and black-and-white James Stewart films. A plasma-screen TV. And silver-framed photographs on the mantelpiece.

Two wedding photographs: the men were obviously Vicky's brothers, because they looked so much like her. Another of Vicky with them both, wearing casual clothes and a mischievous grin. And one of Vicky cuddling a baby.

That was the picture that intrigued him most. Vicky, who said her career meant more to her than anything else, had a look of sheer tenderness on her face as she looked at the child.

A look he could still remember Beth giving him. *The look of a mother.*

'That's my niece,' Vicky said softly. 'My

goddaughter. Chloë Victoria Radley. She's four months old.'

He glanced at her, and there was the same expression on her face as there was in the photograph. That was when he knew. Vicky wanted it all. She wanted her career *and* a family, but she thought she couldn't have it. That she had to give something up.

Maybe he could show her that she didn't have to. That she could have it all.

'She's beautiful.' Like her aunt. 'Anything I can do to help with dinner?' he asked.

'Open the wine?' she suggested.

He just hoped he wouldn't spill it all over the table. Wine, coffee and even mineral water wouldn't be good for the polished surface. But then they were sitting opposite each other. She'd lit a candle—a vanilla-scented candle, just like he'd lit when she'd had dinner at his flat—and a Mozart piano sonata was playing softly.

She lifted her glass. 'Well. Cheers.'

'Cheers.'

The first course dispelled his nerves. Melba toast and fish pâté. 'Mackerel and…?' He couldn't quite place the other taste.

'Horseradish.'

Bought from some upmarket deli?

'It's our cook's favourite recipe,' she said, surprising him. 'She taught me how to make it.'

'You made this yourself?'

'Yes.' She looked slightly offended.

Then he realised what she'd done, and chuckled. 'You wanted to prove you're a better cook than I am.'

She flushed. 'No, I didn't.'

'Yes, you did. You've got a competitive streak a mile wide.'

'Don't be ridiculous.'

Though he could see the glitter in her eyes. Anger? No. Unshed tears. He stopped teasing her. 'You don't have to prove anything to me,' he said softly. Hell, if this table wasn't so wide, he'd reach across and take her hand. 'And you don't need to compete with me either. We're a team.' Weren't they?

She said nothing, but cleared the table ready for the next course. Melt-in-the-mouth beef Stroganoff with baby steamed vegetables—and the rice was moulded in a dome, instead of being spread as a bed for the Stroganoff.

'Did you ever think about becoming a chef?' Jake asked.

'No.'

'Your brasserie would have a waiting list of six months, if not longer. This is seriously good.'

'Thank you.'

She was obviously as ill at ease as he was. Tonight, Jake thought, he'd go home before coffee. Give her space.

Then she produced strawberries dipped in white chocolate, and all his good intentions went out of the window.

'You are a woman well above all lesser mortals,' Jake said after the first taste. 'And white chocolate, since it doesn't contain catechins or any cocoa solids whatsoever, is incredibly bad for you. It shouldn't even be classified as chocolate. So I think I should eat all of them to save you the health risks.' He snaffled the crystal bowl and set it in place of the white porcelain dish she'd given him.

Vicky looked at him in outrage. 'You can't do that! You're supposed to share. And I made *loads*.'

He tipped his head on one side. 'If you want to share, you'll have to come here.'

'That's blackmail.'

In answer, he ate another strawberry. 'Mmm. Perfection. Sweet, juicy strawberries.' Strawberries he'd like to plaster to her skin and lick off.

'Jake…'

He moved his chair back slightly. 'We've barely managed to talk tonight. We're both…I dunno. Ill at ease. Scared. Thinking there's a huge distance between us.' There was—in the shape of her enormous dining table—and this was the only way he could think of to bridge it. 'So let's make it easier on both of us. Come and sit with me.' He opened his arms to her.

She blinked. 'You want me to sit on your lap?'

'Yes. And I'll feed you your fair share of these.' He ate another strawberry. 'On the other hand, you could stay there and watch me scoff these all by myself.'

As he'd hoped, she walked round to his side of the table. She stood by his chair, as if not sure what to do next, so he made the decision for her. He pulled her onto his lap and swivelled her round so she had to put one arm round his neck for balance.

'That's better.' He kissed her bare shoulder.

Lord, her skin was soft. Sweet. 'I've missed holding you. And you're the Honourable Victoria tonight. Aloof and very, very aristocratic.'

She looked away. 'I told you I was rubbish at this relationship thing.'

He pulled her closer. 'That makes two of us, then. Because I haven't a clue what I'm doing. I'm spouting rubbish. I think my brain cells have fried.'

'That's anatomically impossible.'

He laughed. His beautiful, clever lover. So precise. So gorgeous. Unable to resist, he kissed her shoulder again. 'I can't think straight. All I know is I want to be with you. Close to you.' He hummed the Carpenters song at her.

'Oh, that's corny.'

He laughed. 'I know. But it made you smile, so it achieved its point.' He selected a strawberry and drew it along her lower lip. He allowed her to take a bite, then deliberately ate the other half.

'Hang on—that was mine!'

'Ours,' he corrected. 'And this is bliss. Just what I needed after today.'

'Rough shift?'

He nodded. 'I had to give a diagnosis today. Multiple sclerosis.'

'Ouch.'

'Yep. Classic presentation—male, early thirties, had had pins and needles for a while. He's a computer programmer, so he assumed it was repetitive strain injury and he just needed to adjust his working position and do a few hand and wrist exercises. But then he started training for a marathon and he noticed the pins and needles had spread—and they were worse when he'd been training. His legs were weak, even though he'd been working on his muscles.' Jake sighed. 'Then he admitted he'd had a few vision problems. They'd stopped so he assumed it was just because he'd spent too long working at a screen.'

'But it was actually a previous MS episode,' Vicky said.

Jake nodded. 'The MRI scan showed lesions.' He ate another strawberry, to take the bad taste from his mouth. 'He and his wife were just about to start trying for a baby.'

'That's sad,' Vicky said.

Jake nodded. 'He didn't take the news well. He

said he wanted a divorce—he doesn't want to be a burden to his wife, and he wants her to have the family she's dreamed about.'

'That's how I'd be,' Vicky said immediately. 'I'd want to give the one I loved a chance to find happiness with someone else, instead of dragging him down so he was my full-time carer.'

Jake shook his head. 'That's not what a relationship's about. For richer, for poorer, in sickness and in health. You know as well as I do that MS means remissions as well as relapses.'

'But gradually the remissions become incomplete and disability sets in. With every episode, he'll need more and more help. Eventually, he'll need full-time care. It'd be very hard on his wife, looking after a baby *and* looking after him. She'd be under a hell of a strain. All that responsibility and no help.' Vicky raised an eyebrow. 'Plus, if motor symptoms—like weakness in the leg—come at an early stage, the prognosis is poor. If the GP suggested MS to him when he was referred here, and he's a computer whiz. you can bet he looked it up on the Internet and worked it all out for himself.'

'And also worked out the worst-case scenario—which is exactly what you've just given. I know MS isn't curable at the moment, but there's a lot we can do. Interferon, for starters.'

'I know.' She stroked his hair. 'But I still agree with your patient. I'd want my partner to have good memories of me, not wear himself out and then only be able to remember the bad times, the strain of caring for me.'

'But supposing your partner wanted to be there for you? Supposing your partner didn't want anyone else—he only wanted you?'

'I'd walk away,' Vicky said simply.

A muscle flickered in Jake's jaw. 'That takes the choice away from your partner.'

'No. It's practical. It's the way that's going to hurt least, in the long run.' She paused. 'What would you do, then?'

Jake was silent for a while. She had a point. Be with the one you love for the limited time you had left together and make the most of it, or walk away so they could remember you at your best, not when you were in pain and you were both worn out with trying? 'I don't know,' he said finally. 'It's something I hope I never have to deal with.' He could cope with being a carer. He already knew that, from the short time he'd cared for his grandmother. But being the one who was cared for... That would be so much harder. Losing your independence—a gradual erosion, one tiny part of a task at a time. And seeing your partner look at you in a different way—more like a parent than a lover. No longer equals.

It would be hell.

And to see his patient's hopes smashed beyond repair today—because Jake couldn't offer a full and permanent cure—had been tough. Even though he knew nobody could do more than he'd done, Jake had felt as if he'd failed as a doctor.

Vicky kissed the frown from his forehead. 'If I'd known your day was that rough, I'd have made you a cake.'

'Next time, I'll tell you earlier.' He breathed in her scent. 'And now I'm depressing you. So I'll shut up and go home.'

He was miserable. Hurting, because he felt he'd failed. Just as she would have felt in his position.

She, too, hated cases where current medicine just wasn't good enough. Which was one of the reasons why she so wanted to blaze a trail and find solutions. To make things right.

She rubbed her cheek against his. 'Stay. We haven't finished dinner yet. There's still cheese and biscuits. And coffee and petits fours.'

'Home-made petits fours?' he asked, sounding hopeful.

'No,' she admitted. 'I didn't have time to make them.'

He smiled. 'And that annoys you.'

'Well, yes,' she admitted.

'You like things to be perfect. And done your way.' He rubbed his thumb along her lower lip. 'Control freak.'

He didn't sound as if he was sneering. Teasing, yes. But there was affection in his tone, and that made all the difference. 'A bit,' she admitted.

'And honest with it.' He kissed her lightly. 'Thank you for dinner. But I don't want to outstay my welcome.'

'You're not outstaying your welcome.' She'd originally planned to tell him tonight that they could only be friends. But when she was sitting on his lap like this, with her arms round his neck and his arms round her waist… No. Friends, colleagues wasn't nearly enough.

And she'd known that the moment she'd bought a small box at the supermarket that afternoon— without so much as a blush at the checkout. 'Stay awhile,' she said softly, and lowered her head to kiss him.

Kissing Jake definitely ranked up there with one of life's best pleasures. His mouth was so responsive, by turns teasing and provoking and demanding. She could have kissed him all night…except she wanted more.

She felt a slight tug at her hair, and then he'd removed the pins and let her hair tumble down.

'I love your hair loose. It's glorious. All soft and silky and—oh, your hair drives me crazy.' He kissed her throat. 'These are in the way,' he said, gently stroking the pearls.

It was a second's work to remove them and leave them in the middle of the table.

'Better,' he said, and kissed his way along the exact line where the pearls had been. 'Vicky. Tell me to stop,' he whispered as he nuzzled the sensitive cord at the side of her neck.

'Why?'

'I wasn't planning to seduce you tonight. I'm not…prepared.'

So he hadn't taken her for granted. It made her glow with pleasure. 'Just as well I am, then,' she said coolly.

He jerked back, and looked her straight in the eye. 'You bought condoms?'

She flushed. 'And now you think I'm a tart.'

A slow, sexy smile spread across his face. 'No way. I think you're a fairy godmother. Though, um, I rather liked Vicky the Bad Girl.'

She kissed him again. 'If you were thinking of the table, my bed's more comfortable.'

He raised an eyebrow. 'You didn't show me your bedroom.'

'Because I didn't want you thinking I was making any assumptions. And because I wanted dinner, first.'

'You said we hadn't finished dinner,' he reminded her.

She grinned. 'Who says we have to eat it here?' She slid off his lap and held her hand out.

He stood up and let her lead him to her room. When she opened the door, he sucked in a breath. 'You sleep in a four-poster?'

'Um, yes. Look, it's family furniture. I inherited it. But the mattress is fairly new.'

'A real four-poster.' Though he sounded intrigued. A quick glance at his face told her he wasn't sneering: he was delighted. 'A princess's boudoir.'

Dark wood—though she hadn't used heavy velvet drapes. She'd used filmy white and gold voile, to keep her bedroom light and airy. And when she lit the tealight candles scattered around her bedroom, it did make her feel a bit like a princess in a fairy-tale.

'Candlelight suits you,' he said huskily. 'Do you have any idea how beautiful you look? My raven-haired princess.'

'I'm not a princess. Just an Hon.,' she corrected. 'And I prefer my work title.'

'You're still a princess to me, Dr Radley.' He stepped forward, then bent his head to kiss her again.

The next thing she knew, they were on her bed.

Naked. She couldn't remember taking his clothes off—or him taking hers off. All she'd been aware of was Jake kissing her, touching her, stroking her…and how good it felt.

'It's your boudoir, so you're in charge,' he said, rolling over and pulling her on top of him.

She grinned. 'Now you mention it…' She leaned over to take the box from the top drawer of her bedside cabinet. Removed a foil square. Kissed her way down his body. Teased him with the tip of her tongue, until he was gripping the pillow and shuddering and clearly on the edge of losing his control.

'Ready?' she asked.

'Oh, yes.' Jake's voice was slurred with passion, and it thrilled her to think she could turn this clever, capable man into mush like this.

She unwrapped the condom and unrolled it over his penis.

'Now,' he said, and she lowered herself onto him.

# CHAPTER TEN

VICKY fed Jake another strawberry, teasing him by making him stretch up for it.

'You'll pay for this tomorrow night,' he warned. 'I'll make you beg before I let you have a single chocolate from that box you bought me.'

Tomorrow night. Ah. 'I can't see you tomorrow night.'

His shoulders sagged in disappointment. 'Why not?'

'I'm working.'

'You're on a late?'

'Studying,' she explained.

He shrugged. 'You can study at my place, if you like. And I'll give you a neck massage afterwards, while I ask you lots of awkward technical questions.'

She was sure he was teasing her, then a glance

at his face told her that he was serious. 'You're going to test me?'

'Mmm. I've still got my notes from my last set of exams—I'll dig them out, because you might find them useful. And I have some excellent case studies.'

'I can't study at your house.'

'Of course you can.' He smiled at her. 'I know there's not as much room at my place as there is here, but you can work in my living room. There's a phone point there if you need Internet access. If you want to work in complete silence, just shut the door and I'll cook dinner very quietly. Or if you like to study to music, you'll find something on my shelves. I'm not going to distract you—though I am going to limit you to two hours.'

'Two hours?' She always studied for four.

'And you have to have a five-minute break every half an hour to stretch your muscles. You'll focus better that way.'

It sounded as if he had it all planned out. And she'd been going to tell him it was over. She sighed, and flopped back against the pillows. 'I feel a complete bitch.'

'Why? I know studying's important to you. I told you I'd support you—and I will.'

'I was going to tell you it was over tonight.'

'Uh-huh.' He stroked her hip.

She knew exactly what he wasn't saying: *she* was the one who'd suggested going to her bedroom. 'I'm not good at relationships.'

'You're doing just fine.' He smiled at her. 'It's early days. We still have a lot to learn about each other. But let's take it as it comes. Have fun.'

'Yes.' He was right. 'For once in my life, I'm not going to plan. I'm just going to let this happen.'

'Good.' He fed her a strawberry. 'So it's a date?'

'Sure.' She smiled back at him. 'It's a date.'

For the next three months, Vicky was happier than she could ever remember. She loved her job, and for the first time her family seemed a lot more settled. Seb and Alyssa were besotted with Chloë, who was just starting to rock on her hands and knees. Sophie and Charlie had just announced that they were expecting their first baby. When she took an impulsive trip to Weston, for once she didn't feel Mara's usual chilly disappointment with her—it was almost as if her mother accepted the choices she'd made. And, best of all, she had Jake.

All was very right with Vicky's world.

Jake had introduced her to new things. To sitting on a beach and watching the stars on a summer evening. To eating popcorn at the cinema—to her delight, he enjoyed old films as much as she did and had found some tiny arthouse cinemas where they showed classics rather than the latest releases. To walking barefoot on the grass at Kew.

He'd kept his word about not standing in the way of her career. Some weekends she found herself studying at the finish line of a half-marathon after cheering him off at the start, or at an airfield while she waited for him to drop out of a plane. Other weekends, he dropped her off at the local university library, then met her and took her back to his flat where dinner was waiting for her. And she'd helped him make up some fiendish quizzes, and baked cakes for a fundraiser for him.

He'd said right from the start that they were a team. Vicky had never been a team player; she'd always been on the sidelines, and she'd thought she preferred the head-on challenges of chess or tennis. But with Jake, she found she liked being part of a team—at work *and* at home. She'd even relaxed enough to let Jake stay overnight in her flat. He kept a toothbrush and a razor in her bathroom, and a change of clothes in her wardrobe. Just as she kept a toothbrush and a change of clothes at his place. The few nights they didn't spend together now, she found herself missing him.

Though they hadn't actually declared their feelings for each other, Vicky knew Jake loved her. It was the little things he did. The way he'd find her an unusual brain scan to look at, or cook her a special meal, or play one of her favourite pieces of music on his piano. He'd even shared his mother's tapes with her—and Beth Lewis singing 'Moon River' had brought tears to Vicky's eyes. The first song Jake had ever hummed to her had been one that *meant* something to him.

Jake loved her. And she…she loved him. He made her feel complete. Three-dimensional. Real. And tonight, she was going to tell him. Three little words that she found so hard to say. But Jake was different. Jake was the one she wanted to say them to. Just in case she chickened out, she'd bought him something. A box of five hand-piped chocolates with a very, very special message. She would also say that she wanted to go public. That she didn't care if the whole hospital talked about them. She loved him, he loved her, and everything was going to be fine.

Vicky was in the middle of paperwork when the pain hit. It couldn't be a tension headache—Jake had given her a massage last night and had worked out all the knots in the muscles in her neck and shoulders. Maybe she'd just been studying too hard. Or playing too hard—sleep hadn't exactly been top of her agenda for a while. Her mouth curved at the thought. She'd made love more times with Jake in a week than she had in the previous year before she'd met him. And it was good.

She took a couple of paracetamol, loosened her hair and massaged her scalp to improve the blood flow to it. Half an hour and the pain would be gone. She knew the drill—she'd had a few head-aches lately. It was probably her body's way of telling her to get a bit more sleep, that was all. And in the meantime, she had paperwork to do.

\* \* \*

'So Mr Platt hasn't turned up.' Jake frowned. 'Any message?'

'Nothing,' his secretary said.

'I'll take five minutes, then give him a ring.' He'd booked to review Mr Platt's medication for Parkinson's. Though his patient had had great difficulty even admitting that there was anything wrong—and Jake's gut feeling was that Mr Platt was suffering with depression, a condition that often ran alongside Parkinson's. Maybe a tactful call would help—if he could get the man in to see him, they could talk it over and he could reassure Mr Platt that the way he was feeling right now was very common. And, better still, that he could do something about it.

But there was no reply from Mr Platt's home number. It was smack in the middle of morning surgery time for most family doctors, so Jake knew there was no point in calling Mr Platt's GP for a quick discussion. Instead, he wrote a quick email to the GP, outlining the situation and giving some times when he'd be available for a telephone discussion. His clinic was running ahead of time, so he decided to take a very, very quick break.

Vicky's office door was closed—obviously, she was up to her eyes in paperwork. He wouldn't keep her long—just long enough to tempt her into having lunch with him today. He smiled at the thought, and rapped on the door.

'Come in,' she called.

He closed the door behind him, and the smile faded from his face. Maybe he was imagining it…but she looked very, very pale, and she seemed to be having trouble focusing on her computer screen.

'Jake? I thought you were in clinic.'

'Had a no-show, so I thought I'd come and see my favourite registrar and see if she fancied having lunch with me,' he said. 'Don't yell at me for fussing, but you look a bit pale. Are you feeling OK?'

'Fine.'

Her tone was flat and he didn't believe her. 'Headache?'

'Mmm.'

'Have you taken something for it?'

'Paracetamol, an hour ago.'

And she still had a headache? He frowned.

'You've been getting a lot of headaches lately, Vic.' She hadn't even mentioned them, let alone made a fuss, but he'd noticed her taking paracetamol.

She gave him half a grin. 'I'm probably just sleep-deprived.'

Yes, and he knew why. Because their 'early nights' always turned into late ones—they couldn't keep their hands off each other. But that half-smile bothered him. It was as if she was making the effort but the pain was too much for her.

'Have you always had a lot of headaches?' he asked.

'Stop *fussing*.'

'I will if you answer the question.'

She sighed. 'No. Just lately. I just need to get more sleep.'

A warning bell rang in the back of his head. She'd just started having a lot of headaches… 'Have you had your eyes checked lately?'

'Six months ago—and I have perfect vision.'

So it wasn't that she needed glasses. 'Where's the pain?'

'All over,' she admitted.

'Let me check you out.'

She flapped a hand at him. 'It's just a headache, Jake. Stop fussing.'

He folded his arms. 'You've been having a lot of headaches lately. And it's not usual for you. So I'd be happier if I checked you out.'

She scoffed. 'Don't be ridiculous.'

He growled in frustration. 'This is stupid. I'm in the middle of clinic. I've got patients waiting to see me.'

'Then go back to them and let me get on with this mountain of paperwork.'

'Not until you've let me give you a quick once-over.'

'It's just a headache.'

He didn't think it was.

And she must have guessed what he was thinking, because her mouth compressed. 'Jake, don't be ridiculous. I don't have an aneurysm. You're just seeing things that aren't there because we discussed aneurysms last night. It's like—oh, when medical students first learn about a disease and then panic themselves when they think they might have the symptoms. We're both old enough and experienced enough to know better.'

'Let me check you out. If I'm wrong, there's no harm done—and I'll grovel for the next six months.'

'You're not going to shut up, are you?'

'No.'

She sighed. 'All right. You've got five minutes.'

But the quick neurological tests had him worried. 'There's a hole in the middle of your visual field.'

'No, there isn't.'

'Vicky, get out of denial. I'm not happy about this.'

She scowled. 'Jake, you're overreacting.'

'You've got a bad headache. You don't normally get headaches but you've had several recently—a lot, I'd say. You've got a hole in your visual field. And don't argue—you turned your head so you could read the middle letters.' He paused. 'Does this feel like the worst headache you've ever had in your life?'

'No, it *doesn't*. There's nothing clinically wrong with me. The paracetamol will kick in shortly.'

It should have kicked in already. But obviously she wasn't going to listen to him. Time to compromise. 'You've got until lunchtime. Until I've finished my clinic,' Jake said. 'And if the headache hasn't gone, I want you to have a scan.'

She flapped a hand at him. 'Jake, I don't have a family history of aneurysms. I don't smoke, I don't drink to excess, and I don't have any medical conditions.' She ran through the list they'd gone through together last night. 'No polycystic kidney disease, no Marfan syndrome, no connective tissue disorders, no neurofibromatosis. My cholesterol levels are fine. My blood pressure's slightly on the high side, yes, but it runs in the family and I'm taking diuretics to keep it under control—and, yes, before you ask, I take my medication properly. I do *not* have an aneurysm!' she said, gritting her teeth.

But Jake couldn't leave it. 'You know as well as I do that aneurysms are symptomless for a long time. This might be the first symptom. A sentinel headache.'

'*If* it's an aneurysm—and I don't think for one moment it is—it hasn't ruptured so a CT scan won't show anything. Neither will a lumbar puncture, so don't you dare suggest sticking needles in me.'

'MRA, then.' Magnetic resonance angiography was non-invasive, and could show up unruptured aneurysms. However, they both knew the scan wasn't good enough to help plan surgery. If it showed anything, they'd need to do more tests. Something involving a contrast dye—something that carried a risk.

'You're making a fuss over nothing,' she insisted.

He wasn't backing down. 'Lunchtime. And you have to be honest with me. Otherwise, I'll drag you off to Radiology myself. Kicking and screaming over my shoulder, if need be.'

Her expression told him she realised he meant it, and to hell with hospital gossip. 'All right. Lunchtime. But my headache will be gone by then,' Vicky insisted.

'Lunchtime. And I'll track you down if you disappear without seeing me,' Jake warned.

'You're fussing over nothing.' She waved her hand as if shooing him away. 'Go and finish your clinic.'

'Lunchtime,' Jake said warningly.


Vicky continued with her paperwork. Though she found herself squinting at the computer screen.

A hole in her visual field.

Was Jake right? Was she really turning her head to see better, without realising it?

No. She was perfectly all right.

Though when Jake walked into her office at lunchtime—without knocking, this time—she had to admit the headache was still bad.

'Radiology. Now.'

'Jake, there are such things as queues.'

'This is an urgent referral. Hell, if I have to, I'll pay for it to be done privately, here and now.'

Her chin came up. 'I can afford to pay my own way.'

'I know. Your bank account's a lot healthier than mine. But...' He shook his head in seeming exasperation. 'Vicky, I'm worried about you. Seriously worried. And I'm damned well not going to let anything happen to the woman I love. Not when I can do something about it.'

She stared at him in shock. He'd said it. *The woman I love.*

'Jake?'

He stared at her, unsmiling. 'Yes?'

'I...' She couldn't say it. Not when he looked

so serious. As if he was scared spitless and was putting a brave face on.

'Radiology,' he said softly. He took her hand and tugged her out of her chair. 'We'll do the questions on the way in. Any metals in your body?'

'Just fillings.'

'OK, they don't count. Any bullet or shrapnel in your body?'

'No.'

'Joint replacement?'

'No.'

'Any drug allergies?'

'No.'

'Any chance you could be pregnant?'

They'd been careful. 'I don't think so.'

'You can do a test while I'm filling out the questionnaire. Just to be safe.'

And what if she was pregnant? What then? She pushed the thought away. That was more than she could deal with right now. 'You're being very bossy.'

He stopped in mid-stride. 'Because I've got a gut feeling about this, and it isn't good. Now, will you please answer the questions? Claustrophobia?'

'No. And I know what the procedure involves. I've referred patients myself.'

'That isn't the same as going through it yourself.'

She knew that. Did he think she was stupid? She was about to yell at him when she saw the worry etched in his face. No, he didn't think she was stupid. He was being abrupt because he was panicking. 'Jake, we can't queue-jump.'

'We're not. They're expecting you.'

'You *what*?'

'Not *you* you,' he added. 'I said I might have a patient with an urgent referral. And that I'd ring down if I didn't need the procedure.'

He was serious. He really, really did think something was wrong. Ice trickled down her spine. 'Jake…if they find something…'

'Then we'll deal with it.' He put his arm round her shoulders. 'I'm not going anywhere. I love you.'

What a place to say those three little words for the first time. In the middle of a corridor in the hospital, heading towards Radiology. Towards something that could change everything. 'If your hunch is right, I want you to walk away.'

'No chance. If my hunch is right, we can do something about it before anything bad happens.'

*Before anything bad happens.* Nausea roiled in her stomach. 'I'm scared, Jake.'

'I know. But I'm here. They won't let me in there with you while they're doing the scan, but I'll be waiting right next to the radiologist. The second the scanner's switched off, I'll be there.'

The pregnancy test was negative, and Vicky felt oddly disappointed. Then she was cross with herself. They hadn't even talked about having children, let alone planned to have a baby, and now most definitely wouldn't be a good time anyways. She checked the answers Jake had given for her, signed the form, then handed him her watch—the only jewellery she ever wore at work—and the lanyard containing her hospital ID card.

'I'll take care of these for you,' Jake said.

His eyes said the rest of it. *And I'll take care of you.*

No. It was equals or nothing. If the scan was positive, she'd walk away. She wasn't going to drag him down with her. And she wasn't going to tell him she loved him until she knew there was nothing wrong with her. Emotional blackmail wasn't her style—she'd seen Mara do it too often. No way would Vicky ever copy her mother's behaviour.

Almost mechanically, she walked over to the scanner. Lay on the hard narrow bed. Checked that she could see the radiologist in the mirror over her chest. Closed her eyes as the scanner bed moved backwards into the tube. Waited for the pulsing, knocking sounds to start, the noise to signal that the magnetic field was moving over her in the first of the imaging sequences.

Please, don't let there be anything wrong.

Please.

# CHAPTER ELEVEN

THE second the scanner stopped humming, the door opened and Jake was right by Vicky's side to help her off the narrow scanner bed.

'Well?'

'They're sending the results up to my computer.'

She knew he'd been sitting right next to the radiologist, watching the screen over her shoulder. So she also knew he'd seen the results. If they'd been negative, he would have said so. He would have picked her up, twirled her round and said everything was fine. He would have been smiling.

Right now his face was a mask and his words were carefully measured.

Which meant there *was* a problem.

Everything froze. She couldn't remember how to speak. How to walk. But somehow Jake was there, strapping her watch back on her wrist, putting her identity card round her neck again and supporting her out of Radiology.

She had no idea if anyone spoke to her. She didn't hear them if they did. Couldn't hear anything. Just a weird humming, as if she was still lying in the middle of the huge circular magnet.

It took her a while to realise that they were sitting on a bench in the hospital grounds. 'I thought we were going to your office?' she asked shakily.

'No, I thought we needed some fresh air.'

'But…' He had a clinic to run. So did she. They must have been in Radiology for forty minutes. So they were going to be late and—

'Vicky,' he said softly.

Her stomach lurched. 'You saw the results, didn't you?'

'Yeah.'

He wasn't telling her anything. He wasn't saying what she needed to hear—that he'd overreacted and he would grovel for the next six months.

Which meant he'd been right.

She had a cerebral aneurysm—where the wall of one of the blood vessels in her brain had become weakened and started to balloon outwards.

As it stretched, the wall would become thinner and thinner until finally it burst.

'How big?' she whispered.

'Twelve millimetres.'

Anything over ten millimetres had a larger risk of bursting, causing a bleed inside the brain. She knew the stats. Forty per cent of people with a ruptured aneurysm died within the first month. Another third survived but had residual nervous system problems—long-term memory, thinking, perception and even carrying out simple everyday tasks could be difficult. She swallowed. 'So my career's over.'

'No, of course it's not. It's an *unruptured* aneurysm, Vicky.'

So life could carry on as normal. Except she had a time bomb in her head. Every drop of blood that pulsed through it would cause the swelling to grow, just the tiniest fraction. It would get bigger and bigger, until it was pressing on her brain and causing symptoms.

And then it would burst.

'You need to think about how you want to handle this,' he said softly.

'I can't...' She could barely get the words out. 'I can't think straight.'

'Vicky, it's a hell of a thing to take in.' He held her close. 'And you don't have to make a decision today. I think you should take the rest of the afternoon off.'

'I've got a clinic.'

'I'll get cover.'

'You think I can't work?'

'I wouldn't expect *anybody* to work after news like that. You need some time to come to terms with this.' He raked a hand through his hair. 'I don't want you to be on your own, but I've got wall-to-wall patients this afternoon.' He shook himself. 'I'll cancel them.'

'You can't cancel your patients,' she said immediately.

'Watch me,' he said grimly.

She placed a hand on his chest. 'No. I don't *want* you to cancel your patients for me. I'll be fine.' Even though it meant she was going to have to walk away from him—and break her heart in the process. She couldn't expect him to stay with her now. They didn't have a 'tomorrow' any more.

'Can I ring one of your brothers?' he asked.

'No. Charlie'll probably be in Theatre and Seb'll be knee-deep in a trauma case.' And she didn't want them to know. Didn't want them to make a fuss.

'How about your sister-in-law, the one with the baby? Will she still be on maternity leave?'

Yes—but if she told Alyssa, Alyssa would tell Seb. 'I'll be fine.'

'What about your mum?'

'My mother,' Vicky said icily, 'is the last person I'd want around me.' At his look of surprise, she added, 'Your mum might have been wonderful. Not all mums are.' Hers certainly wasn't. Mara would either make a fuss that Vicky was inconveniencing her, or use it as an excuse to be a drama queen and weep all over the place so she was the centre of attention.

'I'm sorry.' His dark eyes were inexpressibly sad.

'I'll be fine.'

Jake took his keys from his pocket and offered them to her. 'Go to my place. It's nearer. And I'll bring us a take-away later.'

She didn't take the keys. 'I don't think I could eat. Look, I'll be fine at my place.'

'Please, go to mine. Do whatever you want. Play my piano—' he'd started teaching her, and she could pick out simple tunes now '—read my books, curl up in bed and have a nap… Ah, hell, I'm coming home with you.'

'No.' And his flat wasn't her home, anyways.

At the look of hurt on his face, she added, 'You don't have a TV. I'm going to spend the afternoon on my sofa watching old Audrey Hepburn films.'

'It's going to be OK, Vicky. We're going to get through this. Together.'

'You're late for clinic. Better go.'

He held her close, as if not wanting to let her go. 'I love you, Vicky. And you're going to be fine. I promise you.'

'Go back to work.' She wasn't going to say it back. Not until she knew she could do it as his equal.

'I'll be with you as soon as I can. And I'll bring dinner home with me.'

Home? But…she wasn't going to his flat.

'Home's where you are,' he said softly. 'Whether it's a mansion flat or a stately home or a studio apartment no bigger than a cupboard. Or even a cave at the top of a mountain. Like it or not, Vicky Radley—now I've said it, I'm going to keep saying it. I love you.'

Saying it until he wore her resistance down. If only he knew how much she wanted to say it, too. But she wasn't going to. Not until she'd thought about how to deal with this.

She went back to her place and ignored the messages Jake texted her between every patient. She just needed to think.

She put *Breakfast at Tiffany's*, one of her favourite films, on the DVD player, but she couldn't concentrate. It didn't make her smile the way it usually did.

An unruptured aneurysm.

She could just leave it. Watch and wait. The risk of rupture for an asymptomatic aneurysm was about one or two per cent a year—whereas the risk of dying in surgery was about three and a half per cent.

Current surgical thinking was that anyone with a life expectancy of more than three years would be better off having an operation. She was thirty-one. With a life expectancy of another fifty years. So if she wasn't having symptoms from the aneurysm, the stats should point her towards an operation.

Except hers wasn't symptomless. There was a hole in her visual field. And the headache could be a prodromal headache—thought to be caused by a small leak of blood that didn't cause the aneurysm to rupture, it was a warning sign of an impending rupture. Sometimes it appeared two weeks before the aneurysm burst.

*Two weeks.*

If she left it to rupture… There was a huge risk of a rebleed after it had settled. Up to fifty per cent of ruptured aneurysms burst again in the first two weeks—and the chance of dying was around eighty-five per cent. Scarily high.

So there was no choice. She'd have to have an operation. Which meant another decision: clip or coil? Clipping meant placing a surgical clip around the neck of the aneurysm—it stopped blood flowing into the aneurysm, removing the risk of it rupturing and letting blood seep into the brain, but didn't block any other blood vessels. Coiling meant using a soft platinum coil, which was guided into the aneurysm and caused a clot to form inside; the clot blocked the aneurysm from the rest of the circulation and meant it was less likely to rupture. The risks were lower than that of surgery, but it was a newish procedure and the long-term outcome wasn't known.

Facts. She couldn't make a decision until she knew the facts. She paused the film, switched on her laptop, flicked into her Internet connection and started researching the online medical journals. She'd subscribed to the main ones in her field, so there was no problem accessing research papers. Microcoils and aneurysms… The studies so far showed that they worked best on smaller aneurysms, and there was a chance of the aneurysms recurring.

So the choice was obvious. Surgery. A clip. And as soon as possible.

The second she cut the Internet connection, her phone rang. She knew who it would be before she answered. Really, she should start cooling things off between them. But her hand seemed to have other ideas and picked up the phone.

'Been on the Net?' Jake asked.

'How did you know?'

'Your landline was busy and you weren't answering your texts.' He paused. 'I've been doing the same. Want to compare notes over dinner?'

As if they were discussing a patient... Trust Jake to know how she needed to deal with this. Professionally. At a distance. He wasn't trying to smother her or panic her. 'Sure.'

'Thai, Chinese, pizza or Indian?' Jake asked.

'Whatever's nearest.'

'OK. Thai. See you in half an hour?'

'Fine.' She could cope if he kept things like this. Light. Not intense.

Vicky was curled up on the sofa watching the rest of *Breakfast at Tiffany's* when he pressed the intercom. She dragged herself off the sofa and pressed the answering switch to let him in, then left her front door open and curled up on the sofa again.

'Hey, beautiful.' He was carrying a huge bouquet as well as a brown paper carrier bag full of Thai food.

It was the flowers that did it.

*Flowers.*

What people gave at funerals.

She started to cry.

\* \* \*

Jake *knew* he should have cancelled his list that afternoon. And this proved it. With a muffled curse, he set the food and flowers on the floor, joined her on the sofa and pulled her onto his lap. He held her close, stroking her hair and letting her howl into his chest.

When her shudders died down—and the front of his shirt was soaked—he pulled back far enough so he could kiss her forehead and the tip of her nose.

'I'm sorry,' she choked. 'I'm being stupid.'

'No, you're not.' He stroked her cheek. 'You're human. And you've had a nasty shock today.' He swallowed. 'A shock that was all my fault. I panicked and bullied you into having that scan.'

'I'm glad you did. Otherwise…'

She let the sentence trail off but he knew what she meant. Otherwise, the aneurysm could have ruptured—and the chances were she wouldn't have survived the rupture.

'Hey. It's not going to happen. We know about it and we can do something about it.'

'But you bought me flowers.'

'To cheer you up.'

'People give flowers at…' She closed her eyes, clearly unable to form the rest of the sentence, and a single tear leaked from her eyes.

He kissed it away, guessing what she'd thought. People gave flowers when you were really ill and they didn't know what else to do. And at funerals. 'People give flowers at happy times,' he said softly. 'For birthdays and red-letter days, and just to say I love you.' There were flowers everywhere at weddings, too—not that he was going to say that right now. She wouldn't be receptive to *that* idea. 'And to make you feel good when you're having a bad day—like today. It's kind of a visual hug.'

'A visual hug.'

'No orchids. I got you gerberas and freesias and all sorts of things. Things that look pretty, things that smell nice. Come and help me put them in water.' Vicky was a practical person. Doing something would help—he'd already left her on her own to brood for far too long. 'Plus, dinner's getting cold.'

'And your shirt's wet.'

He brushed a gentle kiss over her lips. 'You can get me out of my clothes any time you want, sweetheart.'

'How about now?' she asked shakily.

Affirming life. Yeah. He could understand that. 'I'm in your hands.'

With trembling hands, she undid his tie and dropped it in the middle of the floor. She undid the buttons of his shirt and slid her hands across his pectorals, before easing the fabric off his shoulders and dropping it to the floor.

'Jake. I need you,' she whispered.

She still wouldn't say the L word. OK. 'Need' would have to do for now. Jake stood up, took her hand and let her lead him to her bedroom. Slowly, tenderly he undressed her, kissed every piece of skin he uncovered and buried his face in her hair. Her beautiful, long hair that smelled of vanilla. A lump blocked his throat: in a few days' time, her hair would be gone. Shaved off.

*If* she agreed to the operation.

And even then there were no guarantees. The unthinkable could still happen. He'd jinxed her by falling in love with her—he'd loved his mother and his grandmother and he'd lost them. And now he could lose Vicky.

'Jake.' She kissed him as if it were the last time.

It couldn't be. He wouldn't *let* it be the last time. She was going to be fine.

But he was especially gentle when he touched her. Stroked her all over. Kissed his way down her spine. Rolled her over onto her back and knelt between her thighs. Protected her. And slid deep, deep inside her.

It was more intense than anything he'd ever known, as if his body had suddenly become super-sensitive. Her scent filled his head. He could hear every breath—he was sure he could even hear her heart beating. And touch…every brush of her skin against his set his nerve-endings aflame.

When her body rippled around his, he buried his face in her shoulder. 'I love you, Vicky,' he whispered.

She wouldn't say it back. He knew that. But it was all right: she didn't have to say it to feel it. And, right now, as his climax answered hers, he was sure that she felt it just as deeply as he did.

They'd find a way. Just holding her close in silence was enough for now.

Some time later, her stomach rumbled.

'Dinner's cold, but I could reheat it in the microwave,' he suggested.

'Don't you dare. Reheating take-away leftovers is the quickest way to get food poisoning. And I need you to be well.'

He frowned. 'How do you mean?'

'Because,' Vicky said, 'I decided this afternoon. I thought about the stats. I can't just watch and wait with this—this *thing* in my head. My neurological status is excellent. And if there is a tiny bleed, then my H and H scale has to be the lowest possible score.' The Hess and Hunt scale—usually shortened by surgeons to 'H and H'—graded the clinical condition of a patient with a bleed into the brain. The lower the score, the better the patient's condition and the better the chances were.

'And clipping's safer than coiling for someone of my age,' she added.

She was going to have the operation…so did this mean she'd actually let him look after her? Considering the conversation they'd had about his MS patient only a couple of months before, he was surprised. He'd thought she'd be more likely to push him away. Thank God she was seeing sense. 'I agree. And it's up to you whether you want to stay at my place or for me to stay here until you've recovered.'

'Neither.'

'What?' He was having difficulty following this conversation. 'But…you're going to need someone to look after you when you're out of Intensive Care. Or were you planning to go back to your mother's?'

'No.' She rolled her eyes. 'For someone so bright, you can be remarkably dense. Jake, I want you to do the op.'

# CHAPTER TWELVE

SHE wanted *him* to do it?

How the hell could he stand in Theatre with the woman he loved on the operating table in front of him and cut into her brain? 'No.'

'What do you mean, no?' Vicky stared at him. 'You've done the operation before—you know how to free the neck of the aneurysm from the feeding vessels without rupturing it so you can put a clip round it. You're familiar with microsurgical techniques. I've seen you work, Jake. I even know how neatly you close incisions.'

He closed his eyes for a moment. 'I can't do it on ethical grounds. I'm involved with you, Vicky.'

'There isn't a hospital policy about not being able to operate on family members or people you're involved with. Well…not that I can think of. And we've kept it quiet about seeing each other, anyways. So you won't get into trouble.'

'I don't give a damn about getting into trouble. I'm saying that I'm involved with you so I can't be detached enough.'

'That's an easy one to solve.' She folded her arms. 'As from now, we're history.'

Considering that they were in bed together, naked... He shook his head. 'No, we're not. And even if you go through with dumping me, it's not going to stop me being in love with you. I can't operate on you, Vicky.'

She tightened her arms, and he realised that she was shaking and trying to pretend she wasn't. 'Ah, Vicky. Don't do this.' He put his arms round her, holding her close against him again. 'I love you. And it's not over between us until you look me in the eye, tell me you don't give a damn about me and mean it.'

She was still shaking. 'I don't give a damn about you.'

'Look me in the eye and say that,' he challenged softly.

But although she twisted round to face him, she

didn't say it. He didn't gloat. He just kissed her. He needed to feel her mouth on his, feel her breasts pressed against his chest and her heart beating.

'I love you. And nothing's going to change that,' he said softly when he broke the kiss.

'Then do this for me. Please.' Her breath hitched. 'If I have this operation, I need to be in the hands of someone I trust. Someone I trust with my future career—someone I trust with my whole life.'

She'd said she needed him. Trusted him. But she still hadn't used the L word. He tried, very hard, not to mind.

'If you loved me,' she said very softly, pulling back from him, '*really* loved me, you'd do it.'

'I do really love you—and *that's* why I *can't* do it. I told you, I can't be detached enough. I can't be a surgeon and pretend it's just another operation on my list and make what might be a really tough clinical decision when it's the woman I love under my knife. If it…' The thought was unbearable. His voice cracked. 'If it goes wrong, how would I ever live with myself?'

'It won't go wrong. I believe in you.' She paused. 'If you let someone else do it, and it goes wrong, won't you always be asking yourself, "What if?" Won't you ask yourself if you could have done it better—done it *right*?'

Of course he would, and they both knew it. 'You're playing dirty.'

'I know. And I'm sorry.'

He could see that on her face. Guilt mixed with fear and pleading. Yet she wasn't the guilty one— he was. He gathered her to him. 'It's all my fault.'

'How do you work that out?'

'I'm a jinx. I loved my mum and dad. They died. I loved my nan. She died. I love you, and…' The words stuck in his throat. Choking him. Oh, God. Please, don't let this be happening. Please, let it all be a bad dream. Please, let him wake up and find he was just in Vicky's arms and everything was just how it had been yesterday morning.

She took his hands and pulled back from him slightly. 'Look at me, Jake Lewis. Look me in the eye. You're *not* a jinx. Your mum and dad died, yes—but it was an accident. You were twelve at the time and you were on another continent!

How could you possibly have had anything to do with it? And your nan… You know the stats. Strokes happen. The risks increase with age. She was—how old?'

'Seventy.'

'Seventy. It wasn't your fault.' She paused. 'Look at it another way. If it's a jinx, then this is third time lucky. Because, this time, you can do something about it. You're here, now, right in the thick of it. You can fix this.'

Or make it worse. 'I need to think about this.'

'It's the only way.'

'Give me time, Vicky,' he said hoarsely. 'Please.'

'Sure. We won't talk about it any more tonight.' She kissed him lightly. 'Let's go and make dinner together. And I'm sorry I, um, wasted the take-away.'

'It was mutual.' He smiled wryly. 'And you're just a little bit more important than a brown paper bag full of food.'

'I'm glad to hear it.'

'Even if it was red chicken curry with sticky jasmine rice,' he added, teasing her.

She groaned. 'Don't tell me you bought those tiny little spring rolls.'

The ones he knew she adored. 'Yup. And yellow tiger prawns.'

She looked rueful. 'I've got the ingredients for omelette and salad. Doesn't quite compare, does it?'

He stroked her face. Nothing compared to *her*. 'Stay here. I'll make it.'

'No, we'll do it together. You do the omelette, I'll do the salad.'

'Fine.'

But Jake could barely concentrate in the kitchen. He burned the first omelette he made, and Vicky took over. 'Before you set my smoke alarm off and panic the whole building,' she said with a grin. 'And to think *I'm* supposed to be the one with the field-of-vision defect.'

'Not funny.' He stood behind her as she deftly whisked the eggs, with his arms wrapped round her waist and his face buried in her hair. This couldn't be happening. Shouldn't be happening. And he was supposed to be strong for her right now, even though he wanted to crawl into a corner and weep.

The omelette—even though it was light and fluffy

and filled with melted Brie—tasted like ashes. And although Vicky didn't mention the issue between them, it was still there. Getting bigger and bigger. Damned if he did, damned if he didn't…

'Sleep on it,' she said softly.

'What?'

'You don't want to talk about it. So sleep on it.'

He nodded. 'I'd better go home and let you get some rest.'

'I don't think I want to be on my own.' She rested her head on his shoulder. 'Stay with me tonight?'

'Of course.' Though he didn't sleep. He just lay there and listened to Vicky's quiet, even breathing. Wishing he knew what was the right thing to do.

Jake was on early shift again the next morning. Vicky, under protest, agreed to spend the day with her feet up and not to study. Somehow he made it through the day. But instead of going straight to Vicky's flat after his shift, he took the tube to Walthamstow, bought flowers from the market and a bottle of water and went to the cemetery.

There, among the Victorian white stone angels, he had a place to think.

Mechanically, he walked to his grandmother's grave. *Lily Lewis. Rest in Peace.* A peace Jake was very far from feeling right now.

'I don't know what to do, Nan,' he said as he took the previous week's flowers from the vase on her grave and wrapped them in the paper from the fresh flowers. He rinsed out the vase, filled it with water again, and started threading red carnations into it.

'If I do it and I make a mess of it, she could die— or be left needing a lot of care. She won't be able to be a neurologist any more. And she'll never forgive me for taking her career away—I'll lose her.' He added more carnations. 'But if I don't do it, she'll never forgive me for backing away when she needs me most. And I'll lose her.' He swore softly. 'Sorry, Nan. You'd wash my mouth out with soap for that. It's just I don't want to lose her, but I can't see any way out of this. Whatever I do, it's going to end up in a mess.'

He knew his grandmother couldn't answer him—and how he missed Lily's common sense— but it made him feel better just saying the words aloud. 'I've done the operation before. I'm a good surgeon, Nan. If she was anybody else, I'd say yes without any hesitation. I'd do it, and I'd do it well. But she matters, Nan. She really matters. I'd walk to the end of the earth for her. Over hot coals, broken glass, anything.' He swallowed hard. 'But I'm so scared I won't be able to do this. She wants me to operate on her. How can I, when I'm involved with her? I have to be detached, see her as just another patient. And she's not. She's the woman I want to spend the rest of my life with. I can't do it.'

Vicky had given him her spare key so he didn't have to bother with the intercom. When he walked into the flat, he could hear music from the living room. She was watching another old film—this time *High Society*. The irony was like a fist in his gut. The rich society girl and the boy from the wrong side of town. True love. Just like them.

But it wasn't going to work out for them like it did in the movies.

He pushed the thought aside and pinned a smile to his face. For Vicky's sake, he was going to be strong. Someone she could lean on.

'Hey.' She smiled up at him. 'How was your day?'

'Fine. You?'

'Bored to tears. Because someone made me promise I'd do nothing all day—and I keep my promises.' She rolled her eyes. 'Next time you hear me moaning on the ward that we're rushed off our feet and I could do with sitting down for a minute, remind me of today.'

'Sure.' He sat next to her and kissed her lightly. 'Sorry I'm a bit late. I put some flowers on Nan's grave.'

Vicky knew what that meant. Jake had been thinking. He'd admitted to her a while back that he always went to his Nan's grave whenever he wasn't sure about something; she'd been pretty sure he'd go there today. So had he reached a decision about the operation?

She was careful not to push him. She just took his hand and squeezed it. 'You miss her a lot, don't you?'

'Yes. She would've liked you.'

'I'm sure I would have liked her. Everything you've told me about her…she sounds lovely.' The kind of grandmother—or mother—everyone would want. Full of common sense and good advice and a hug when you needed it most. Behind you all the way. The kind of mother Mara never could be.

Jake said nothing, so she waited. He'd tell her when he was ready.

And then it came. The answer she'd been praying for. 'I'll do it.'

'You'll do it?' She needed to be sure. Sure she wasn't just hearing what she wanted to hear.

'Yes. But there's something I want you to think about. You're literally putting your life in my hands. If I make the tiniest slip, you could die.' He looked grim. 'And brain surgery's not without risks. You could have a stroke. Be left paralysed, unable to talk. Your memory could be affected. At the very least, you could have some neurological deficits after the op.'

'I know. But you could say the same about any other surgeon. I want *you* to do it—I trust you.'

He nodded. 'You're asking me to do something incredibly hard, something I don't want to do—and do it because I love you. The stakes are high, Vicky. Really high. If I don't do it, I lose you. If I do it, and something goes wrong, I lose you.'

'Nothing's going to go wrong.'

'You don't know that for sure.' He looked brooding. 'Vicky, I love you. And that's why I'm going to do it, if you still want me to. But if you put me through this, you don't get to walk away afterwards. I want you to marry me.'

'So the stakes are as high for me as they are for you?' she guessed.

'Yes.' The word came out as an anguished whisper.

She knew she was asking a lot of him. She wasn't sure if she could do it, if their positions were reversed: could she perform a life-saving operation on him, knowing that one slip of the scalpel, one wrong move with a retractor, could cause permanent and severe damage?

And now he was asking a lot of her. Marriage. When he knew that her career came first, last and always.

It had, before today.

But things were different now. She'd been doing a lot of thinking. And if she pulled through the operation—then, yes. Jake was the one she wanted to spend her life with. Marry. Maybe have children with, if they were lucky. 'You get me through this unscathed, and I'll marry you any time, any place you choose. But if it goes wrong, I want you to walk away and forget me.'

'I can't do that.'

'Yes, you can. I'm a neurologist. I know the risks. I've got a four per cent chance of dying on the table. The aneurysm's unlikely to grow back, but it could burst during the operation—and if there's a massive bleed into my brain I could have a stroke. Or if you catch a major artery during the op, or clip the parent blood vessel by mistake, it could make me have a stroke. But I know you're careful, Jake. Your stats are good. I think everything's going to be fine.' She paused. 'But if it isn't…if I do have a stroke and need long-term care, I need you to walk away. Don't you see? Right now, you want to look after me. But there won't be any respite. Day in, day out. Maybe for years and years and years. And eventually you'll start to resent it. Then guilt will set in. And slowly, slowly, what you feel for me won't be love any more. It'll be pity. And you'll hate yourself for it.'

'It doesn't have to be like that.' He raked his hand through his hair. 'I cared for Nan.'

'But it wasn't for very long. And it wasn't full time, either, because she made you promise you wouldn't give up your studies.' She knew she was ripping his scars wide open by reminding him of past pain, and she hated herself for it. But he had to be realistic about things, see the situation for what it was. 'Jake, I'm thirty-one. We could be talking about forty, fifty years. That's a hell of a long time.'

'I know it's a long time. Marriage is forever. The stakes are high for us both.' He sighed. 'I was so sure you'd say no.'

And that was why he'd asked her, because he'd wanted her to refuse the deal? Or did he really want to marry her? He'd already said he loved her, and she believed him. She knew, too, exactly how much she was asking of him. And that reminded her of something she needed to say. 'If I hadn't been ill…I was going to tell you yesterday. Except I thought I might chicken out.'

'Chicken out of what?'

'There's a box in my desk. Flat, gold, with a dark green ribbon round it. It's for you. A present.'

He frowned. 'It's not my birthday.'

'Unbirthday present. Except I didn't get the chance to give it to you.' She smiled. 'I'll give it to you tomorrow.'

He shook his head. 'You're not going back to work tomorrow.'

'I'm bored stiff hanging around here all day. I'd rather be doing something to keep my mind off it.'

'No.'

'Jake, be reasonable. I'm supposed to avoid stress, right?'

'Which is why you're not doing a shift on a busy ward that's short-staffed right now.'

'Has it ever occurred to you,' she asked quietly, 'that it's more stressful for me doing nothing? Jake, I'm used to hard work. It doesn't bother me. I like being busy. But if I have to sit around and do nothing for the next week, I'll go crazy. That's *my* definition of stress. Please. I want to go in tomorrow.'

'What shift are you supposed to be on?'

'Late. Same as you.'

'OK. But if you feel the slightest bit rough,' Jake warned, 'you stop.'

'All right.'

'Promise?'

'Promise.'

'So what were you going to tell me?' he asked.

She smiled. 'Tomorrow.'

'Why not now?'

'Because,' she said softly, 'I need to believe tomorrow's going to come.'

He flinched and she stroked his face. 'I'm going to be all right, Jake. Because you're going to do the operation. And you're the best neurosurgeon I know.' He just had to believe it, too.

And maybe tomorrow, she'd be able to convince him.


Jake put his head round Vicky's door at four o'clock the following afternoon. 'How are you doing?'

'OK. Got a minute?'

'Sure.' He closed the door behind him.

She took the box from her drawer and handed it to him. 'This is what I was telling you about.'

Nothing on the wrapping gave him a clue about what it was.

'Remember, I bought it the day before yesterday. Before I knew about the aneurysm.'

Slowly, he undid the dark green bow. Took the

lid off. And stared in surprise. A row of five hand-made chocolates. With a message piped on the top: V R ™ J L.

'I was going to tell you the other day. But then this all blew up. And I didn't…' She closed her eyes for a moment. Please, let him believe she was telling the truth. 'I don't want you to think I'm only saying it now to make you operate. Because I'm not. And you can ring the chocolatier and check when I ordered this, if you don't believe me.'

He still hadn't spoken. And she couldn't read his thoughts from his face. He just looked stunned. Shocked.

Or maybe he didn't believe what he was reading. He'd said it enough to her, over the last day or so. Maybe it was time she said the words. Words she'd never, ever thought she'd say to anyone. 'I love you, Jake Lewis. With all my heart.'

# CHAPTER THIRTEEN

SHE loved him. *She loved him.*

Jake was unable to speak. He just held her close, his face against her hair. He wasn't dreaming. She'd said it. The Honourable Victoria Radley loved Jake Lewis. And she'd written it in chocolate.

'We're going to get through this, Jake,' she said softly. 'You're going to operate. I'm still going to be professor. And life's going to be just as it was—just as it was before we knew about the aneurysm.'

His heart contracted sharply. He wanted to tell her not to make plans, not to jinx it. Just in case.

'And we're going to get married. We're going to have it all,' she said.

Was that too greedy, asking for way too much? 'I'd settle for getting you safely through next week,' he said softly. He pulled back slightly and kissed her on the tip of her nose. 'You're going to have to tell the ward about the aneurysm,' he warned. 'You can't just let them find out about it when you turn up in here next week as a patient.'

'Or on your operating table.'

Mmm, and he still wasn't a hundred per cent happy about that. 'When are you going to tell them?'

She sighed. 'All right, don't nag. I'll tell them tomorrow. But if anyone pities me or starts treating me like a delicate little flower…'

He laughed. 'They wouldn't dare. But people care about you, you know. They're a bit in awe of you, but they care.'

'Mmm.'

She looked uncomfortable. Why didn't she like people making a fuss over her? From the photographs on her mantelpiece—and the fact that she saw her brothers at least once a week—he knew she was close to Seb and Charlie. But he'd bet that she hadn't said a word to them either. 'Have you told your family yet?'

'No.'

'Don't you think they'd want to know?'

'They'll fuss. And I'm already having to put up with enough fussing from you.' She narrowed her eyes at him. 'I'll tell them the day before the op.'

'That's not fair, Vicky. It's dropping a bombshell on them. Give them a few days to get used to the idea.'

'No. They'll fuss.'

She refused to discuss it further, so Jake took matters into his own hands. That evening, when she was asleep, he borrowed her mobile phone from her handbag, copied down the two numbers he wanted and made the calls.

The next morning, he told Vicky he'd be late back after his shift because he needed to see someone. To his relief, she assumed it was a fundraising thing for the Lily Lewis Unit and didn't suggest joining him.

When he walked into the bar, he recognised Charlie and Seb immediately. Even if he hadn't seen their photographs, he'd have known who they were because of the family resemblance. The same aristocratic bone structure, dark hair and slate-blue eyes. They looked so much like Vicky, it hurt.

He went over to them and introduced himself.

'So what's this about?' Seb asked. 'You said you didn't want to talk about it on the phone.'

Straight to the point. Just like Vicky. 'There isn't an easy way to say this.' So he'd be blunt, too. 'Vicky needs an operation.'

'And you're breaching patient confidentiality?' Seb asked.

Jake grimaced. 'I'm telling you as her next of kin.'

'Are you her doctor?' Charlie asked.

She really had kept him quiet. Jake sighed inwardly. She'd said she loved him—but clearly not enough to tell her brothers about him. 'Yes and no. She wants me to perform the operation.'

'So what's the problem? I assume you're her colleague, so is it because you know her from the hospital?' Seb asked.

'No,' Jake said quietly, 'it's because she's my girlfriend.'

'Your *girlfriend*?' The brothers spoke in unison, and both of them sat up straighter and looked very hard at Jake. If it hadn't been for the circumstances, he would have been amused. Vicky didn't need her brothers to protect her from him. She was more than capable of holding her own.

'How long has this been going on?' Seb demanded.

The relationship? 'A few months.'

Seb's eyes narrowed. 'She hasn't mentioned you to us. At all.'

'She wouldn't,' Jake said. 'You two have been trying to pair her off at dinner parties and driving her mad. If she'd told you about me, you'd have insisted on meeting me and giving me the once-over. Especially given who she is and the fact that I come from a very different background. So you may as well know now. I'm a consultant neurologist at the Albert Memorial Hospital, but I don't come from a rich family. I rent a very, very small flat. And I don't give a damn about Vicky's money or her rank or her property. It's irrelevant.'

Charlie assessed him, then nodded. 'She did the same to us. Gave Sophie and Alyssa the once-over, I mean.'

'Rest assured, I'm never going to hurt Vicky,' Jake said wearily. 'I love her, God help me. But I'm seriously not happy about doing this operation.'

'So what exactly is wrong with her?' Charlie asked.

'Cerebral aneurysm. Twelve millimetres. She needs clip ligation,' Jake said quietly.

'Hell.' Seb put his hand over his mouth. 'I had no idea.'

'Neither did she until this week—when she got what I think was a sentinel headache.'

'You mean, it could rupture at any time?' Charlie raked a shaking hand through his hair. 'Why the hell didn't she tell us?'

'Because she says you'll fuss. But I'm not happy. So I pinched her mobile phone to get your numbers.' Jake paused. 'I, um, haven't said anything to your mother.'

'Don't,' Seb said feelingly. 'We'll deal with *her*. Vic doesn't need Mama Dearest on her back. Not at a time like this.' He shook his head. 'I don't believe this. Our baby sister's got a life-threatening condition and she hasn't breathed a word to either of us.' He stared at Jake. 'Was she actually going to tell us?'

Jake nodded. 'She planned to do it the day before the op. But I said you needed a bit more time to come to terms with it.'

'Too bloody right,' Seb said. 'I'll kill her.'

'No, you won't.' Charlie put a hand on his shoulder. 'I'm the oldest. *I'll* do it.'

'She needs you,' Jake cut in. 'Both of you. Though she won't admit it. And whatever you do, don't take her flowers.'

'Why not?' Seb asked, lifting his chin and looking every inch the aristocrat, disdainful and irritated by some commoner telling him what to do.

'Because I did,' Jake said softly. 'It made her cry. And that's when she told me she wanted me to do the op.'

'How good are you?' Seb asked.

'If Vic wants him to do it, he's good,' Charlie said, before Jake could answer. 'She's picky.'

'You can say that again.' Jake took a deep breath. 'There's something else you need to know.'

'More?' Seb closed his eyes. 'I'm not sure I'm ready to hear this.'

'I've asked your sister to marry me. And she said yes.'

'*Vicky?*' Charlie looked shocked. 'Vicky's going to marry you?'

'I'm not holding her to it,' Jake said dryly. 'She

asked me to do something tough—operate on her—so I've asked her to do something tough, too.'

'So you're blackmailing her into marriage,' Seb said, giving Jake his iciest glare.

Jake sighed. 'No. I love her. I want to marry her—or just live with her for the rest of our lives. A piece of paper isn't going to change the way I feel about her. But you know Vicky. She's got her heart set on being a professor of neurology before anything else happens in her life. I wanted to show her how high the stakes were for me. Because if this is what she wants from me, I damn well want everything from her.'

'If she agreed to marry you in order to get you to operate, you must be seriously good,' Seb said. 'So I'm with Vic. I want you to operate.'

'It's not ethical. Not when I'm involved with her,' Jake said. 'Would you operate on your wife?' He remembered that Seb was an emergency specialist. 'OK. Suppose your wife had been in an accident. She has flail chest, a tension pneumothorax and she's in VF. Would you work on her or get someone else to do it?'

'I'd do it,' Seb said without hesitating. 'Because I'd want to know she'd get the best possible care. The way *I'd* do it.'

'Me, too,' Charlie said. 'If Vicky wants you, so do I.' He gave Jake an assessing stare. 'Does Vicky love you?'

'Yes.'

'That's the important thing.' Charlie held out his hand. 'I guess this is welcome to the family.'

Jake shook his hand solemnly. 'Thank you.'

'Though I wish it had been in better circumstances.' Charlie took a deep breath. 'Where is she?'

'Home. Her flat, that is,' Jake said.

'Right. I think we need to pay our baby brain surgeon a visit—don't you?' Seb asked.

'Definitely,' Charlie agreed.

'Go easy on her,' Jake warned. 'Stress isn't going to help.' He folded his arms. 'I think I'd better go with you.'

To his surprise, Charlie burst out laughing. 'Listen to us. As if Vicky needs protecting from any of us. She's probably more scary than the three of us put together.'

'We're not going to yell at her,' Seb promised. 'Though I think she's going to yell at *you*, Jake, when we turn up.'

She did. 'Who the hell do you think you are, interfering like this?' she demanded.

'Jake Lewis, consultant neurologist,' he retorted.

'Before you go off at the deep end, Vic, he's right. We needed to know,' Charlie said, giving her a hug.

'And we're on your side about him doing the operation, so don't yell at *us*,' Seb added. 'In fact, you should be grovelling and thanking us profusely for nagging him into it.'

'You said you were meeting someone,' Vicky accused Jake.

'I was.'

'You lied.'

He shook his head. 'Absolutely not. I just didn't say who I was meeting.'

'It was a lie of omission. You *knew* I thought it was something to do with fundraising for the unit.'

Jake shrugged. 'So sue me.'

Her eyes narrowed. 'How did you get their numbers?'

'Your mobile phone.'

She stared at him in outrage. 'When?'

'When you were asleep.' Jake took a chance, and gave her a sidelong look. 'You always fall asleep after sex.'

Vicky turned absolutely bright red.

Charlie hooted. 'Oh, this more than makes up for the way you grilled Sophie.'

'And Alyssa,' Seb added, laughing. 'In fact...' He whipped out his mobile phone and took a photograph. 'Proof that Queenie actually blushes.'

'I've told you before, don't call me that stupid name. And I'm going to kill all three of you,' Vicky said through gritted teeth.

'No, you're not. Because otherwise who's going to do the operation and sit with you in Intensive Care afterwards?' Charlie asked.

'I hate you.'

'No, you don't.' Seb ruffled her hair. 'And, for your information, squirt, we're here because we love you. And we both want to be best man, by the way.'

'That's fine by me,' Jake said.

'You told them *that* as well?' Vicky looked at Jake and sat down. 'I give in. Just, please, tell me you didn't ring my mother.'

'No,' he said softly, sitting beside her and taking her hand. 'Just Charlie and Seb. Because you love them. They matter.'

'Yes.' She blinked the tears away. 'Charlie, Seb. I…I didn't know how to tell you.'

'You know we love you. And at least we know now why you've rushed off early every time we've seen you the last few months. I was going to have a word with you about being such a workaholic,' Seb said.

'We both were,' Charlie said. 'We were planning to take you out to dinner and talk some sense into you. Except you kept putting us off and saying you were busy. We thought you were studying, not out playing.'

'Get off my case,' Vicky said. 'I'm doing fine.'

'I'm going to make coffee,' Jake said quietly, and left Vicky alone with her brothers. When he returned, Vicky's eyes were red and Charlie and Seb both had damp lashes. He set the coffee-tray down. 'I'll give you some time,' he said.

'No need,' Charlie said, making room on the sofa next to Vicky. 'You're family.'

Family. Something Jake hadn't had in a long, long time.

They didn't even know him. He was from a different world—he had no idea how you were supposed to address a baron, and he'd probably breached every single rule of etiquette going since he'd met Charlie and Seb. And yet here they were, accepting him. Saying he was one of them. *Family*.

So now there were four people he couldn't let down next week. Vicky, her brothers and himself.

To stop himself thinking about it, he switched into work mode. 'Do you both have high blood pressure, too?'

Seb and Charlie glanced at each other. 'Uh-oh, Vic's found a male version of herself,' Seb said.

'A workaholic,' Charlie agreed.

Jake frowned. 'Seriously. Vicky says the condition runs in the family.'

Charlie nodded. 'But I'm pretty sure I'm fine. *I'm* not the party animal of the family.' He looked pointedly at his brother.

Seb sighed. 'You know very well I've reformed since I met Alyssa. I've cut down hugely on my alcohol intake—and I never smoked, anyways.'

'Our father died of a heart attack,' Charlie said. 'But I'm not aware of any aneurysms in the family. Do you think we should go for screening?'

'Up to you,' Jake said. 'It isn't necessarily a familial condition—but siblings over the age of thirty do have the highest risk. Are either of you prone to headaches?'

Seb shook his head. 'Not me.'

'Nor me,' Charlie said.

'Then it's your choice. I'd suggest an MRI angiogram or helical CT scan every five years, starting now. And you should let your GP know about Vicky, for your records,' Jake added. 'And if either of you get an unusual headache, pain of any sort in your head or eye, or visual disturbances of any kind—floaters, spots, any holes in your visual field—I want you in my department *immediately*.'

'Were you this bossy with Vic?' Seb asked, sounding interested.

'Yes,' Vicky answered with a grimace.

Seb grinned. 'Good. About time you had some of your own medicine. All puns intended.'

'I'm going to be fine,' Vicky said. 'Just…bald.'

She took a deep breath. 'I've had long hair ever since I can remember.'

'Except when you were five and you hacked your fringe with the nail scissors from the bathroom cabinet,' Charlie reminded her. 'You were going to hack the rest of it off if Mara sent you back to ballet lessons.'

'It was my choice,' Vicky said. She lifted her chin. 'And I'm going to cut my hair myself this time. Before it gets shaved off.'

'You don't have to. You know there's a hairsparing technique—we can take just a quarter of an inch along the incision,' Jake reminded her.

'But it's messy. And my hair's really long.'

He knew. He'd spread it over her pillow often enough.

'And if there's a complication… No.' She shook her head. 'It's coming off. All of it.'

Jake groaned. 'Not until you've told the ward. Please.'

'I mean it.'

Her eyes were shining just a little bit too much. He closed his hand around hers. 'Fine. After you've told the ward. And if it bothers you, having your head shaved—you can do mine, too.'

'You'd shave off your hair for me?'

He nodded. 'If it would make you feel better.'

'Supposing, when my hair grows back, it's different?'

Was that what was worrying her? That she'd look different and he'd feel differently about her? His grip on her hand tightened. 'It won't matter.' He loved her hair, yes—but he loved her more. 'It could be bright green and spiky, and it wouldn't matter.'

'Don't give her ideas,' Seb teased. He got to his feet. 'I've already been an hour longer than I told Alyssa I'd be. And it's my turn to get up if Madam wakes in the night, so I'd better get home. But I'm happier knowing you're in good hands.' He kissed his sister. 'Just do what the man tells you, OK?'

'I second that,' Charlie said, giving her a hug. 'And you can expect a visit from Alyssa and Sophie tomorrow. They'll probably ring you to-night, actually. The second after we've told them.'

Vicky sighed. 'I *knew* you'd fuss.'

'We're not going to fuss. But we're your big brothers. We reserve the right to worry,' Seb said. 'We'll see ourselves out. Make sure you get some rest.'

'I hate sitting still, and you know it,' she muttered.

'Tough. Do what your doctor tells you. Jake—good to meet you.' Seb shook Jake's hand. 'Take care of my little sister.'

'I'll take the "or else" as read,' Jake said dryly.

'I don't think we need it,' Charlie said quietly as he, too, shook Jake's hand. 'I can see how you feel about her. It's the way you look at her—the same way I look at Sophie. The same way Seb looks at Alyssa.' He paused. 'You'll keep us informed?'

Jake nodded. 'As soon as I get the op scheduled, I'll let you know. It's up to you if you want to be there.'

'They are *not* observing!' Vicky said, sounding horrified.

'What, not even to check that you do have a brain, squirt?' Seb teased.

'You're welcome in my theatre,' Jake said quietly, 'provided that the patient consents.'

'We'll get Alyssa and Sophie to work on her and make her say yes,' Charlie said.

'And if you still refuse, Vic,' Seb added, 'we'll be waiting outside.'

'It's a four-hour op,' Vicky said. 'Half an hour for anaesthesia, fifteen minutes to position the patient, then inserting the lumbar drain, prepping, three-quarters of an hour to expose the brain, anything up to an hour and a half to target the artery and clip it, an hour's closure, then extubation…' She shook her head. 'You'll go crazy with the wait. Go to work and do something useful.'

Charlie sighed. 'I'm glad I'm not in your shoes, Jake. She's going to be hell as a convalescent.'

*If she made it.*

The words were unspoken, but Jake knew they were all thinking it.

But Vicky was going to make it. She had to make it. Or the sun would stop shining for the rest of his life.

# CHAPTER FOURTEEN

VICKY told her colleagues, one by one, the next morning, and she was near to tears at the end of it. She hadn't thought that people liked her very much. Respected her, yes—she was good at her job. But she wasn't part of the crowd—she never had been, from school onwards. So she really hadn't expected her desk to be covered with cards and little gifts— flowers, chocolates, a paperweight and a magnet with a joky message about working too hard.

The next few days moved with frightening speed. Jake had booked her in for an electrocardiogram, blood tests and a chest X-ray, and pronounced the results as being perfect. There was the dinner that she knew they'd have to go to—so her sisters-in-law could also assess Jake and give him their approval. Though she wasn't surprised that they took to him, because she knew they had a lot in common. It turned out that Jake's school had been just round the corner from Sophie's, and he and Alyssa had both been brought up as only children by a single parent—in Jake's case, his grandmother.

And then it was the day before the operation.

Jake had booked her in for a catheter angiography. 'It's not risk-free,' he reminded her before she signed the consent form. 'You might feel a bit hot and bothered for a moment when the dye goes in, but then you'll be fine.'

She rolled her eyes. 'You don't need to talk me through it. I've booked in patients for these myself. I know how it works and I know the risks of the procedure.'

'That doesn't mean you can sign the consent form without thinking it through,' Jake said. 'I don't want any corner-cutting.'

She sighed. 'Look, you and I both know that using contrast dye in an X-ray is the best way to get a decent picture of my arteries, so we can plan the surgery properly.'

'We?' he queried.

'You don't think I'm going to just sit back and not ask a single question about the X-rays, do you?'

He leaned over to kiss her. 'No. And of course I was going to give you the chance to review the X-rays yourself. But I'm doing the op my way,' he warned.

'As I'll be unconscious throughout it, I don't have much choice,' she grumbled.

But she was glad he came down to the X-ray department with her. She didn't flinch when the local anaesthetic was put in, or when the catheter was threaded into her groin, because Jake was holding her hand all the way through it. A contrast dye was injected through the catheter and the radiographer took several X-rays.

And then they were back in Jake's office, with the films pinned up against the light board to review them.

'Good news,' Jake said lightly. 'There's only one. And it's a saccular aneurysm.' Saccular aneurysms were also known as berry aneurysms because they looked like berries growing on a branch. And it was the easiest form to deal with.

'Which sort of incision are you going to do?' she asked.

'Pterional incision—it's shorter, there's less

trauma to the temporalis muscle, and the bone flap is smaller,' Jake said.

'OK.' She took a pair of scissors from Jake's desk.

'What are you doing?'

'What does it look like?' She cut off a hank of hair.

'Wouldn't you be better off going to a hairdresser?' Jake asked, looking horrified.

'Nope. My problem, my hair, my way.' No way was she going to let anyone else do this. A change like this…it had to come from her. She continued cutting until her hair lay on his desk in a pile. 'How do I look?'

'Lopsided.'

She regretted the impulse now. 'I look terrible, don't I?'

'You look beautiful, but with a truly bad haircut. I don't—' He stopped abruptly.

She knew what he'd been going to say. That he didn't think hairdressing was an alternative career for her. After tomorrow, who knew what she'd be? A neurologist…or an ex-neurologist. Jake's fiancée…or the woman she wanted him to leave behind.

She willed back the tears. Not now. She wasn't going to cry until she knew the worst. And even then, she could deal with it. She was a Radley. Tough. Strong. And she could stand on her own two feet. She'd had to do that for years and years and years.

'Can you get the hair clippers?' she asked.

He nodded. 'Want me to do it for you?'

'I…' She sagged back against his chair. 'May as well. You can see what you're doing better than I can.'

He wasn't gone long. Though it was long enough for her to start brooding.

It must have shown in her face, because he gave her a hug. 'Hey. Bald women are beautiful. There's Sinead O'Connor—she shaved all her hair off and she looked gorgeous.' His lips twitched. 'Though if you start singing like her, I might have some issues.'

'I don't know whether to laugh or cry,' she admitted.

'Smile,' he advised. 'There was this song my mum used to sing. It's on one of her tapes. Nan had a version by Nat King Cole—I remember her telling me it was written by Charlie Chaplin.' He began to croon 'Smile Though Your Heart is Breaking' to her.

She had a feeling he'd played that track a lot after Beth had died. He was word-perfect on it. And when he'd finished singing, he stood back. 'OK. You're even, now.'

She dared not look in a mirror. 'Thank you.'

'You look dignified,' he said softly.

Hideous, more like. And she knew how he loved her hair. Whenever she wore it up, he couldn't resist unpinning it and running his fingers through it or burying his face in it.

Would he ever do that again?

'Vicky? Do something for me?'

'What?'

'Can I…please, can I have a piece?' He lifted up one of the long locks from his desk.

A piece of her hair. Like a memory. Something else you did with dead people.

Again, her thoughts must have been transparent, because he said softly, 'It's traditional for a baby's first haircut. Keeping the first curl. I'm not being morbid.'

'Aren't you?'

He coughed. 'Seb and Charlie want a piece, too. They say it's like your first haircut because your hair's been long ever since they can remember.'

She felt a muscle tighten in her jaw. 'All right. But not until I'm round from the operation. I'll give it to you all myself. Tied in a bright pink ribbon.'

'I can't ask for more than that.' He leaned forward and kissed her. 'Right, now get out of my chair.'

'Why?'

'Because you're doing me, now.' His dark eyes were utterly sincere. 'And you can't shave my hair off when you're sitting and I'm standing.'

His hair. Which always flopped over his forehead and gave him the look of a disreputable cherub. Especially when he'd made love to her. He was really going to let her cut it all off? 'All of it?'

'Uh-huh. And you can have a lock of it, if you're good.'

'People are going to ask you about your hair. They'll gossip.'

He shrugged. 'Let them.'

'No. We agreed, we'll keep quiet about us until after the op.'

'OK. Then I'll do it after the op. As a badge of faith. Or you can do it, if you'd prefer, when you can sit up again.'

'Deal,' she said.

\* \* \*

That night, when they made love, it was with a deeper intensity than Jake had ever experienced. And he knew why: both of them were wondering if it was the last time. Ah, hell. He wished Vicky had kept her hair just a few hours longer. So he could have buried his face in it one last time, smelt that gorgeous vanilla scent.

'Kiss me, Jake,' Vicky whispered.

He did, but he had to blink back tears. This really felt like goodbye. The end of everything.

And that was when he realised how much he loved her. How much she'd become part of his life. And how much they hadn't had time to do—they hadn't danced in the rain or had a snowball fight or shrieked down a roller-coaster together. They hadn't crunched through autumn leaves or chosen a Christmas tree together or seen a thunderstorm or spent a weekend in a cottage by the sea. So many things he wanted to do with her…. Would they ever get the chance?

He slept fitfully that night. And every time he woke, he knew that Vicky was awake, too. And he knew she was pretending to be asleep to make him feel better—just as he was doing, too.

He needed sleep. He had a four-hour operation in front of him. The most important operation he'd ever perform in his entire life. But the waiting…it was like the wait before every exam he'd ever sat, plus his driving test, all rolled into one. Unbearable. This wasn't something he could just resit if the results weren't good: it was a life-or-death situation. And everything depended on his skill.

Finally, it was half past six, and he had an excuse to get up.

'You look like hell,' Vicky said.

'I feel it,' he admitted. 'You?'

'Scared. I'm going under the knife.' She took a deep breath. 'But at least I know it's your knife. So I'm going to get the best possible care.'

'And if…?' He couldn't force the words out.

'If I don't…' She gulped. 'If I don't make it, it won't be because of you. Because I know you'll have done everything I would have done—and you're a better surgeon than I am.'

'Now she tells me.' His vision blurred. 'Oh, hell, Vicky. You *have* to make it. What am I going to do without you?'

'You're not going to be without me. I'll come back and haunt you.'

'Not funny.'

'Hey. If it wouldn't make us late for Theatre, I'd drag you back to bed. But we…' Her breath hitched. 'We have an operation to sort out.'

She let him hold her close. It felt strange, holding Vicky without her hair tumbling down over his arm. But at least he was holding her. Please, please, let her be in his arms tomorrow.

'Come on. I'll make you some breakfast,' she said.

Jake shook his head. 'You're nil by mouth. I'm not mean enough to eat in front of you. And I'm certainly not going to make you cook anything for me.'

'Go and shut yourself in the kitchen, then,' she said. 'You can't operate on an empty stomach. Or without a mug of your disgusting sweet black coffee.'

'I'll make instant so it won't smell so strong,' he promised. 'Vicky. I love you.'

'Me, too.'

But she wouldn't meet his eyes. Ah, hell. She was already going distant on him. Preparing for the worst. She'd told him she wanted him to walk away if it went wrong, but he'd refused to promise. This was one woman he'd never walk away from, come rain or shine or the unthinkable.

He could barely force down the bowl of cereal and mug of coffee. The journey to hospital was hell. And then they were on the ward. Vicky took off her watch and handed it to Jake. 'Keep it safe for me.'

The only jewellery she ever wore, apart from that string of matched pearls with one of her little black dresses.

He'd given her nothing. Not even a cheap pendant. As for an engagement ring…he'd known Vicky wouldn't even consider looking for one until after the operation, so he hadn't pushed her. Now he wished he had.

Silently, he put the watch in his wallet.

The anaesthesiologist came in to talk Vicky through the risks of anaesthesia and surgery and check that she hadn't eaten or drunk anything since midnight.

'Nothing since nine o'clock last night,' Vicky reassured him, and signed the consent form.

And then Jake had to leave her. 'I'll see you in Theatre,' he said quietly.

She nodded. 'And I'll see you when I come round.'

He was scrubbing up when Charlie and Seb walked into the scrub room, dressed in theatre greens.

'Jake.' Charlie smiled at him, but Jake could see the strain in his face. 'Is your offer of observing still open?'

'Of course it is.'

'It isn't that we don't trust you,' Seb added.

'You've already looked up my CV on the hospital intranet,' Jake said, straight-faced.

Seb flushed. 'Well, yes.'

Jake smiled. 'I would've done the same in your shoes. And it's better that you're here, seeing what's happening, instead of waiting outside and counting how many seconds it is since you last looked at the clock.'

Seb looked sombre. 'Yeah. It's bad for you, too.'

Jake nodded. 'But at least it keeps me too busy to worry. And you're right. If someone else had done it, I'd be fretting that I could have done it better.'

'We're not going to make a single comment,' Charlie said. 'Just forget we're there.'

Jake pursed his lips. 'You're plastics and emergency, right? So you've got a working knowledge rather than a specialist knowledge of what happens in neuro.'

Charlie nodded. 'We both mugged up on it over the weekend.'

Jake grinned. 'Good. I can get technical with you, then.'

'How do you mean?' Seb asked.

'I'll talk you through the op. We'll pretend I'm doing a teaching op.' His voice cracked. 'And that the patient's someone else.'

'Hey. She thinks you're the best. We trust her judgement,' Charlie said. 'But thanks. It'd be great if you could talk us through it.'

'Sure.'

Vicky was already under a general anaesthetic when they walked into Theatre, and her head was held in position by a three-pin device. Jake introduced Seb and Charlie to his assistant and the theatre team. This was going to be the hardest operation of his career, but there was no other choice.

'Anyone mind if I have Corelli on while we

work?' he asked. The soothing, regular rhythm would help to keep him calm.

When everyone murmured agreement, he arranged for the music to play softly, prepped the incision area and inserted a lumbar drain into Vicky's lower back. 'This takes out some of the cerebrospinal fluid and lets her brain relax during surgery,' he explained. 'I've put a local anaesthetic into her skin to decrease bleeding—the scalp always bleeds profusely and the bleeding interferes with surgery.' Of course, Charlie and Seb knew that…but he was treating this as a teaching operation, so he may as well go through the whole thing. Plus, oddly enough, it was helping to calm him. Helping him to stay detached. Just as long as he didn't look at Vicky's face.

He made the pterional incision into her skin, exposed the skull, lifted the skin and muscles off the bones and folded it back. 'Now I can see what I'm doing, I'm making burr-holes into her scalp so I can cut a window of bone.' He did so and lifted the flap. 'We'll store this safely until the end of the operation. OK. I'm opening the dura mater, now.' This was the membrane between her brain and her skull. 'I'll fold it back to expose her brain, then I'll use retractors to open up a corridor between her brain and her skull.'

As he started to work with the microscope, he began to relax. He'd done this before. He knew what he was doing. And everything was going to be fine.

'I'm opening the corridor up now and tracing the artery through to the aneurysm. I'm going to control the blood flow to it now—that's so if it *does* rupture when we handle it, we can stop the bleeding instantly.' He checked Vicky's vital signs with the anaesthetist. 'OK. The flow's under control. The aneurysm's held tight by connective tissue, so I need to free it. I want to isolate it from the other structures in the brain, and I need to make sure we don't include any perforators.' Perforators were small arteries.

He held the clip open with a clip applier. 'This is made of MRI-friendly metal. I'm going to place the clip across the neck of the aneurysm and release the jaws; when they close, the aneurysm will be blocked from the parent artery.' He did so and inspected the position of the clip. 'Good. It's not narrowing the parent artery at all, and there are no other arteries inside the clip.' Now for the crunch-time bit. 'Next, I need to puncture the dome of the aneurysm to make sure blood isn't filling it.'

Everything was going according to plan. Though Jake was always meticulous in preparing for surgery, so he wasn't expecting any nasty surprises. 'I'm going to do intra-operative angiography to make sure the blood is flowing correctly through the artery—if it isn't, I can correct it now. If I leave this until after the operation and there's a problem, it means back to Theatre and another anaesthetic, so it's better to do it now.' To his relief, all was well. 'OK. The blood's flowing properly and the clip's in place.' He removed the retractors. 'Now we close the dura. Sutures. Bone flap back in place—secured to the skull with titanium plates and screws. Suture the muscles and skin back together, soft adhesive dressing over the incision…and wait for her to wake up.'

Back in the scrub room, Charlie said, 'Neat work. If you ever fancy switching to plastics…'

Jake smiled and shook his head. 'I like neurology.'

'So what's next?' Seb asked.

'Wait for her to come round,' Jake said. 'She'll be in Intensive Care for a couple of days, then moved up to the ward for the rest of the week.'

'And in the meantime, she's at risk of hydro-cephalus,' Charlie said. Hydrocephalus was an excess amount of cerebrospinal fluid within the skull, and it was a possible complication after brain surgery.

'But she'll be under neuro obs so they'll see if there's any sign of raised intracranial pressure,' Seb said. 'Headache, vomiting, any deteriorating of mental function—and an MRI will show up the excess fluid. A shunt will drain it away safely to the peritoneal cavity.'

Jake grinned. 'Hey. Want to swap jobs?'

Seb shook his head. 'No way. Emergency medicine's a buzz. Neurology is scary. If *I* make a slip, I can fix it. If *you* make a slip...' His voice faded.

'I didn't. It was a textbook op. No complications during surgery.' Jake immediately found a piece of wood to touch. Please, God, don't let there be any post-op problems. 'And, as you said, she'll be under observation. We'll spot the symptoms of early hydrocephalus or vasospasm straight away and deal with it.' Vasospasm was the sudden constriction of a blood vessel, which led to a decrease in blood flow and could lead to a stroke.

'What if you're in Theatre with another patient?' Charlie asked.

'I won't be,' Jake said quietly. 'As of now, I'm off duty until Vicky's out of hospital. I'm here if my locum or anyone on the team needs a second opinion, but I'm not moving from Vicky's bedside. She's my priority.' For now and for always. He took a deep breath. 'Let's go and see if your sister's woken up.'

# CHAPTER FIFTEEN

'HELLO, beautiful. How are you feeling?' Jake asked.

''S if a horse just kicked me in the head,' Vicky mumbled.

'I can give you something for that.'

Vicky's eyelids fluttered and she forced them to stay open. 'How'd it go?'

'Textbook. So you now have a nice MRI-friendly clip sitting in your head.'

'Mmm-hmm.' It was hard to concentrate. She just wanted to go back to sleep.

Jake quickly checked her pulse, temperature and respirations. 'You're doing OK. But you need to tell me if you feel sick, your head hurts or you're in pain.'

'Tell you?'

'Yes. I'm doing your obs.'

'Make a nice nurse.' She tried for a smile. 'Blue dress'll suit you.'

He chuckled. 'Yeah, right! Seb and Charlie want to see you. Do you feel up to it?'

'Mmm.' It was too much effort to force words out.

'I'll take that as a "not really". How about I get them to be porters and wheel you down to ICU?'

'OK.'

They must have been waiting right outside the recovery room, because then they were there by her bed, wheeling her down the corridor.

'Well done, squirt,' Seb said. 'You picked a good surgeon there.'

'And his stitches are as neat as mine,' Charlie said. 'He'll do.'

'Uh-huh.' She couldn't keep her eyes open. But she heard Jake say, 'OK, that's enough. She needs rest. I'm staying with her, so I'll text you both every hour on the hour with an update, and I'll ring you if I'm not happy about anything.'

And then everything faded out.

She woke later in a room she vaguely realised was the intensive care unit. There were cables and catheters everywhere. Her throat felt sore.

'Sweetheart?' Jake's voice. 'Don't try to speak. You've got a nasogastric tube in and I've got you on a trickle of oxygen right now.'

So that was the tight feeling across her face. Oxygen mask.

His fingers gently pressed hers. 'If you're in any pain, just press my hand.'

No. No pain. A dull ache, but nothing to warrant pain relief.

She managed to turn her head towards him. He had what looked like a full day's growth of beard and his scrubs were rumpled. Clearly he'd spent the night at her bedside. Had she been out that long? Or had he kept her lightly sedated to give her body time to recover from the stress of the operation?

'You're doing well,' he said softly. 'We'll have the tubes out tomorrow. Then you'll be back on our ward in a day or so. You'll be home in a week.'

He'd done it. He'd taken the tick out of the time bomb.

She moved the pad of her thumb against his skin. It wasn't enough contact. Not nearly enough. She wanted him to hold her…but she was going to have to wait.

\* \* \*

'She's asleep again,' Jake said to Seb and Charlie. 'She's going to be tired for a while.'

'Make the most of it,' Seb said. 'As soon as she's well enough to go up to the ward, she's going to be a nightmare. She'll smuggle textbooks in. And she'll probably try to sneak into her office and catch up on her paperwork.' His tone was light, but Jake could see the strain in his face.

'She's going to be fine,' he reassured them. 'Go in and see her.' He paused. 'This sounds stupid, because you *know* what ICU's like—but it's different when it's someone close, not a patient. She's got an NG tube in and an oxygen mask, and there are syringe drivers plus monitors for her heart rate and rhythm, blood pressure, central venous pressure and oxygen saturation.'

'And our baby brain surgeon is smack in the middle of it,' Charlie said quietly. 'Have you had a break today?'

'I'm really pleased with her obs,' Jake said, ignoring the question.

Seb sighed. 'You're as bad as she is. Look, we'll

sit with her for a while, Jake. Go and have something to eat and just chill out for half an hour.'

Half an hour? He couldn't stay away from her that long. 'Ten minutes,' Jake said.

'Twenty, and that's a compromise,' Charlie cut in. 'Jake, if you wear yourself out, you won't be able to look after her properly. Which reminds me, we need to start thinking about a rota system to keep an eye on her when she's out of hospital. There's no point in booking a private nurse because Vicky will say she doesn't need looking after and she'll pay her off. But she can't pay *us* off. Between the five of us, we should be able to sort it.'

Jake's surprise clearly showed on his face, because Charlie added, 'You don't think we'd leave it all to you, do you? That's what families are for. Support when the going gets tough.'

He hadn't had a family since Lily's death. This was going to take some getting used to.

'Alyssa's still on maternity leave, so she'll be able to take some day shifts,' Seb said. 'If we synchronise duties, then Charlie, Sophie and I can cover whenever you're in clinic, Jake—and we'll sort something out for weekends to make sure you actually get some sleep.'

Jake stared at them both, too stunned to say anything.

Seb clapped him on the shoulder. 'See? You're tired now. You did the hardest operation of your life this morning, and you've been keeping Vic under continual obs since. It's physically not possible to keep this up for the next week. So we'll sort it as a family. Go. Break. Now,' he added, pointing to the door.

Jake had no idea what he bought from the canteen. He couldn't taste anything. And he added cold water to his coffee so he could drink it straight down and go back to Vicky's bedside. The caffeine was a welcome jolt to his system, but he only realised that he'd bought chocolate when he arrived back at Vicky's beside and Charlie grinned.

'What?'

'Busy medic's standby,' Charlie said, nodding at the choc bar.

'Did you have something to eat?' Seb said.

'Yes, but don't ask me what,' Jake said honestly. 'I didn't even taste it.'

'Stop worrying. She's still asleep, but she's going to be fine,' Seb said. 'She had an excellent surgeon.'

'I'm glad it's over,' Jake admitted. 'And I'm just lucky I didn't hit any complications. I couldn't have lived with myself if anything had happened.'

'And we made it worse, insisting on being there,' Charlie said, wincing.

'I understand. I think I would have done the same if someone else had operated.' He dragged in a breath. 'Though I never, ever want to do an operation like that again. I've never been so scared in my entire life.'

*I'm glad it's over... I've never been so scared in my entire life.* The words echoed in Vicky's head the next morning. Jake was asleep in the chair by her bed. Clearly he hadn't left the hospital last night, either—and he'd broken all the hospital rules by staying there at her bedside. A nurse must have tucked that blanket round him.

A tear trickled down her cheek, and she reached over to touch his hand, needing the contact.

Immediately, he was awake—as with most doctors, years of training and long nights on call had made him able to snatch sleep where he needed to and be awake enough instantly to deal with a patient.

'Hey.' He leaned over to kiss her cheek. 'How are you doing?' He did her observations. 'I'm happy to take this tube out now. Want me to sort it?'

At her nod, he said, 'Close your eyes and relax. I'm going to make this as easy as I can for you.' Gently, he removed the tube.

'Throat hurts,' she whispered.

'It will, to start with.' He poured a small amount of cool water into a glass and handed it to her. 'Small sips. Take it slowly. If you rush, you'll just bring it straight back up.'

At last the dryness in her throat eased, though it still hurt to talk. 'Sorry,' she said.

'What for?'

'Put you in a bad situation. Operating.' *I'm glad it's over… I've never been so scared in my entire life.* She dragged in a breath. 'I was desperate. Shouldn't have said I'd marry you. Not fair.'

He squeezed her hand. 'Hey. The operation's over now. But I won't hold you to your promise. You don't have to marry me.'

Was it her imagination, or did he sound relieved?

And yet she'd thought he really wanted to marry her. Before the op. Had he never truly meant it? What if he'd only said it to put her off having him do the op, and had been appalled when she'd said yes? Had he wanted to withdraw the offer, and only pity had stopped him saying so before now? Or had he simply changed his mind? He'd seen her as a patient—perhaps he couldn't see her as a lover any more. Or perhaps it was because she looked so repulsive now? She didn't dare ask for a mirror. She didn't want to know how bad she looked.

She felt a rush of misery overcome her exhausted brain. Yes, he'd stayed with her last night. But that must have been out of a sense of duty, not because he wanted to be here. And no way was she going to let *that* situation continue. It was going to hurt—God, it was going to hurt—but she was going to let him walk away. Better that than have to live with his pity.

'Must be tired. Stiff. Go and have a proper sleep,' she said.

He shook his head. 'I'm not leaving you.'

'Crowding me.' Far from it. But if he stayed here, she might embarrass herself further. She might beg him to hold her, to love her, the way it had been before the operation. But she'd pushed him too far. Made him do the unthinkable—she'd given him complete responsibility for her life. Too much. 'Need some rest. On my own.'

He looked at her for a moment, then sighed. 'All right. I'll call in later.'

'Bye.' She tried to sound as cool and casual as she could.

'I've still got your watch.'

'Put it in the sister's office. 'S a safe there,' she mumbled.

'OK. If that's what you want.'

No, it wasn't what she wanted. But she wasn't going to tie him to her out of pity.

She closed her eyes and turned her head away, not wanting to see him leave. The quiet click of the door told her that he'd gone. She was on her own.

Been there, done that, could do it again.

Except it felt so much harder than she remembered it.

Jake sighed inwardly as he left the unit. Vicky had been through a four-hour operation—and it was clearly taking its toll on her. She was tired, out of sorts and thoroughly miserable. Flowers weren't allowed in Intensive Care because of the risk of infection, and she wouldn't be up to eating chocolate for a while. So how could he give her a boost?

An engagement ring...but no. He wanted to choose that with her. Besides, the way she was feeling right now, she'd probably think he was pushing her too hard if he gave her a ring. Better to wait.

He'd go back and see her when she'd had a chance to rest. And maybe there was something that would make her stay in hospital that little bit less miserable...

Vicky woke up, her mouth feeling dry. Everything felt too hot. And her head ached. She was about to grope for the buzzer to call a nurse when she remembered. She'd fallen asleep crying. Because she'd pushed Jake away. Too late to do anything about it now.

She turned her head to the side with an effort. His chair was empty. So he'd taken her at her word, then. Part of her had hoped he'd ignore her and just be there anyways when she woke up.

*I won't hold you to your promise. You don't have to marry me.* Ha. In the end, he hadn't been able to get away fast enough. And now he was gone for good.

She swallowed hard and turned her head away again. So she couldn't see the empty space where Jake should have been—and feel it echoing in her heart.

Some time later, she heard the door open quietly. Probably a nurse come to do her obs. Well, she wasn't in the mood for talking. She kept her eyes closed, pretending to be asleep. Felt a hand against her forehead and heard somebody say, 'I'm not happy with her temperature. Better give her something to bring it down.'

Jake? No. She was hallucinating.

There were other noises in the room. More than one person there, then. You were only allowed two at a time in ICU, so who else was in her room? One of her brothers? Except he hadn't spoken or touched her, and she knew that neither Seb nor Charlie would have been able to resist looking at her chart and making some comment or other, or checking her temperature themselves.

'That's brilliant. Thanks a lot, mate. I'll sort the rest of it out when she wakes up.'

It definitely sounded like Jake. But what was he doing here? And what on earth was he talking about?

Footsteps out. Footsteps in—lighter, quicker. One of the nurses. 'Back *again*? Can't get rid of you, I see.' A laugh. 'So how long has Neurology been this dedicated to patient welfare?'

'This one's a special case. The love of my life,' he said softly.

'That explains it, then.' The nurse sounded decidedly sentimental.

*Love of his life?*

But…he'd said she didn't have to marry him. He didn't want to marry her any more—did he?

When the door clicked again, Vicky turned her head to the side and opened one eye. Jake was settled in the chair beside her bed, reading a journal. Such a simple thing. And it made her want to cry.

Something made him look up, and then his eyes widened. 'Vicky? How are you feeling?'

'Horrible,' she whispered.

His face radiated concern. 'Tell me where it hurts,' he said briskly—sounding cool and professional, like a surgeon, but looking distinctly panicky.

'My heart. I thought…I thought you'd gone.'

'You told me to go away because you felt crowded and wanted to rest.'

'I know.' A tear oozed out of one eye, but when she lifted a hand to brush it away she felt the pull of wires and drips. 'I'm stuck here.'

'And you hate it. You hate being fussed over. And you want to be home.' He leaned over and wiped the tear away gently with the tip of his forefinger.

'I didn't think you'd come back.'

He grinned. 'I ligated an aneurysm, not your common sense! You've had four hours of brain surgery. You're bound to feel a bit fragile right now.'

'You said you weren't going to hold me to my promise. To…to…' She couldn't finish the sentence.

'To marry me? I'm not. You're right, I probably wasn't being fair, asking you.' He stroked her face. 'But it doesn't change the way I feel about you. Seb and Charlie grilled me about my intentions, Alyssa gave me a thorough going-over when she asked me to go take a look at baby Chloë, and Soph cornered me in the kitchen when she asked me to help her clear the table. They know I love you to distraction. I thought you knew that, too.'

'Even though I'm bald?'

Jake groaned, and dropped her hand.

She closed her eyes, wishing she hadn't said anything about her hair. Then she heard a swooshing noise she didn't recognise. 'What are you doing?'

'Drawing the blinds.'

'Why?'

'Because, my love, I'm going to be as bald as you if I'm caught doing this. I'll be scalped and probably banned from the whole of this floor. I'm not even supposed to sit on the end of your bed, let alone do this.' He returned to her side, wriggled onto the tiny space at the edge of her bed and put his arms around her.

Holding her. The contact she'd longed for.

'You're supposed to be lying flat, and you're hooked up to a million and one monitors,' he said dryly.

Right now, she didn't care. The world had just become Technicolor again. Jake still loved her.

'I'm sure my neurologist is capable of putting any wires back,' she teased.

He rubbed his nose against hers. 'Sure I am. But I'm not in charge of ICU. If the consultant anaesthetist catches me, he'll have my guts for garters.'

'Live a little. Take the risk.'

'Oh, I will.' He kissed her gently. 'More than that. Now, first of all, you know I don't care about you being bald. It's temporary, but even if it was permanent it wouldn't bother me. I fell in love with you, not your hair. And why on earth did you think I'd gone for good?'

'Because you weren't here when I woke up.' Her voice wobbled, despite herself.

'I was doing something while you were resting. Sorting out the loan of a flatscreen TV and DVD player while you're in here, because I know there's only one thing that keeps you in bed without complaining.' He grinned. 'Well, only one that the ICU consultant will approve of! The other can wait until you're home.'

So he did still want to go to bed with her? And when she'd thought he'd gone for good, he'd just been busy trying to find something to make her convalescence more bearable. Her heart melted. 'Where did you get it?'

'I pinched it from the private ward.'

'You didn't!'

'Borrowed, with permission,' he amended. 'And I nipped into the high street to get you some films to tide you over, until you tell me which ones you want me to pick up from your place.'

He'd arranged all that for her. Without being asked. 'I…I don't know what to say.'

'I have an idea.' He kissed her lightly on the mouth. 'I just want you to say one little word to me. Though this isn't the best of settings. I should be asking you this under a romantic sunset. Or in that place where the sea looks like a staircase to the moon—I found it on the Internet. We could fly over there and I could ask you then.'

'Ask me?' She wasn't quite following the conversation.

'I've asked you before. Except this time there's nothing hanging over our heads. Just you and me. The op's over now. You're not desperate, and I'm not scared out of my wits. So will you marry me,

Victoria Charlotte Radley? Love me for the rest of our days, just like I'll love you?'

She smiled. 'What do you think?'

'I think,' Jake said quietly, 'if you don't tell me you're going to marry me, I'll set your brothers on you. And your sisters-in-law. And they'll nag you and nag you until you say yes.'

'No need.' She stroked his face. 'There's only one man I want to marry. And now I know I'm going to be OK—that I'm your equal, not an invalid who'd have to rely on you to do nearly everything—there's nothing I want more than to be with you. Love you for the rest of our days.'

He coughed. 'You talk too much. I was only looking for one little word. Three letters. Starts with a Y, ends in an S. Middle letter's a vowel.'

She laughed. 'Yes.'

He held her close. 'If you weren't hooked up to all these monitors and supposed to be lying flat anyways, I'd pick you up and whirl you round.'

'We'll take a rain-check. But we'll do it. Because now we've got all the time in the world.' She kissed him. 'And I'll spend every second of it loving you.'

# EPILOGUE

*Two years later*

'SO WHY this sudden yen for the seaside?' Jake asked as they strolled along the seafront at Southend-on-Sea. 'And why here in particular?'

Vicky spread her hands. 'Let's just say I want to be back where we started.'

He frowned. 'That sounds ominous.'

'No. This is where you kissed me for the first time. And we danced on the sand.'

He eyed the crowded beach. 'Not much chance of that today.'

'We ate fish and chips overlooking the sea. And you sang "Moon River" to me.'

'Now, that we *can* do.' He laughed and draped his arm around her shoulders. 'You're getting sentimental in your old age, Mrs Lewis.'

'Mmm. Mrs Lewis.' She savoured the words.

They'd been married for three months; their small wedding had taken place at Weston. Mara, to Vicky's surprise, had taken to Jake, and Jake even seemed to bring out a better side of Barry. Not to mention becoming firm friends with her brothers and persuading them to join him in some of his more athletic fundraising. Seb, predictably, had trained hard enough to make sure he came first out of the three of them in the triathlon they'd entered, though Jake really didn't care as long as they raised plenty of money for the Lily Lewis Unit. And Vicky had been promoted to consultant. Mrs Lewis rather than Dr Lewis. Life didn't get much better than this.

Apart from the little bit of news she was intending to give Jake in a few minutes' time.

'Professor Lewis to be,' he said thoughtfully.

Vicky laughed. 'Not for a while. Though I wrote accepting that part-teaching, part-clinical post this morning.'

He kissed her. 'Good. Though we're going to miss you at Albert's.'

'You don't get rid of me that easily,' she teased.

'Good.' He ran his fingers through the ends of

her hair. 'Have I told you lately that you're beautiful, Mrs Lewis, and I love your hair?'

He'd kept his word about letting her shave his head as soon as she could sit up again after the operation—and he'd kept his head shaven until her hair had grown back properly. And he'd delighted in unpinning her hair on their wedding day—just as she'd delighted in the way he'd reverted to that slightly scruffy, disreputable style. 'Now who's getting sentimental?' she teased. 'Let's go to the end of the pier.' She wrapped an arm round his waist, and they walked along the pier. When they reached the end, she turned to face him. 'Actually, there is something we need to talk about.' She paused. 'This part-time post. It might have to be very part time.'

'How do you mean?' He stiffened. 'You don't think…?'

He didn't voice his fear, but she knew what he meant. Headaches, floaters—any possible sign of a new aneurysm developing and putting pressure on her brain. 'No. And I don't want to go anywhere near an MRI scanner or X-ray machine for the next thirty-four weeks.'

His gaze narrowed, and then he worked it out. 'Six weeks? You're sure?'

'Did the test this morning. That's why I wanted to come here. I wanted to tell you here, in our special place.'

He whooped, picked her up and swung her round. When he set her back on her feet, he was frowning again. 'How are we going to celebrate? You're not touching any shellfish or soft whippy ice cream. Or anything that might have the vaguest hint of raw egg.'

Uh-oh. She was going to be mollycoddled through her entire pregnancy, by the sound of it. Just as Charlie had mollycoddled Sophie and Seb was mollycoddling Alyssa for the second time.

'How about good old-fashioned English strawberries?' she suggested, and beckoned him closer to add in a whisper, 'In bed.'

His dark eyes crinkled at the corners. He was clearly remembering another first. A moment neither of them would ever tire of repeating. 'Perfect. Let's go home.'

# MEDICAL ROMANCE™

## *Large Print*

### *Titles for the next six months…*

### *December*

| | |
|---|---|
| MATERNAL INSTINCT | Caroline Anderson |
| THE DOCTOR'S MARRIAGE WISH | Meredith Webber |
| THE DOCTOR'S PROPOSAL | Marion Lennox |
| THE SURGEON'S PERFECT MATCH | Alison Roberts |
| THE CONSULTANT'S HOMECOMING | Laura Iding |
| A COUNTRY PRACTICE | Abigail Gordon |

### *January*

| | |
|---|---|
| THE MIDWIFE'S SPECIAL DELIVERY | Carol Marinelli |
| A BABY OF HIS OWN | Jennifer Taylor |
| A NURSE WORTH WAITING FOR | Gill Sanderson |
| THE LONDON DOCTOR | Joanna Neil |
| EMERGENCY IN ALASKA | Dianne Drake |
| PREGNANT ON ARRIVAL | Fiona Lowe |

### *February*

| | |
|---|---|
| THE SICILIAN DOCTOR'S PROPOSAL | Sarah Morgan |
| THE FIREFIGHTER'S FIANCÉ | Kate Hardy |
| EMERGENCY BABY | Alison Roberts |
| IN HIS SPECIAL CARE | Lucy Clark |
| BRIDE AT BAY HOSPITAL | Meredith Webber |
| THE FLIGHT DOCTOR'S ENGAGEMENT | Laura Iding |

MILLS & BOON®

Live the emotion

1106 LP 2P P1 Medical

# MEDICAL ROMANCE™

## *Large Print*

### March

| | |
|---|---|
| CARING FOR HIS CHILD | Amy Andrews |
| THE SURGEON'S SPECIAL GIFT | Fiona McArthur |
| A DOCTOR BEYOND COMPARE | Melanie Milburne |
| RESCUED BY MARRIAGE | Dianne Drake |
| THE NURSE'S LONGED-FOR FAMILY | Fiona Lowe |
| HER BABY'S SECRET FATHER | Lynne Marshall |

### April

| | |
|---|---|
| RESCUE AT CRADLE LAKE | Marion Lennox |
| A NIGHT TO REMEMBER | Jennifer Taylor |
| THE DOCTORS' NEW-FOUND FAMILY | Laura MacDonald |
| HER VERY SPECIAL CONSULTANT | Joanna Neil |
| A SURGEON, A MIDWIFE: A FAMILY | Gill Sanderson |
| THE ITALIAN DOCTOR'S BRIDE | Margaret McDonagh |

### May

| | |
|---|---|
| THE CHRISTMAS MARRIAGE RESCUE | Sarah Morgan |
| THEIR CHRISTMAS DREAM COME TRUE | Kate Hardy |
| A MOTHER IN THE MAKING | Emily Forbes |
| THE DOCTOR'S CHRISTMAS PROPOSAL | Laura Iding |
| HER MIRACLE BABY | Fiona Lowe |
| THE DOCTOR'S LONGED-FOR BRIDE | Judy Campbell |

MILLS & BOON®

Live the emotion

1106 LP 2P P2 Medical